THREE TIMES
A BRIDESMAID…

THREE TIMES
A BRIDESMAID...

BY

NICOLA MARSH

™ MILLS & BOON®

First published in Great Britain 2010
Large Print edition 2010
Harlequin Mills & Boon Limited,
Eton House, 18-24 Paradise Road,
Richmond, Surrey TW9 1SR

© Nicola Marsh 2010

ISBN: 978 0 263 21243 3

Harlequin Mills & Boon policy is to use papers that are
natural, renewable and recyclable products and made
from wood grown in sustainable forests. The logging and
manufacturing process conform to the legal environmental
regulations of the country of origin.

Printed and bound in Great Britain
by CPI Antony Rowe, Chippenham, Wiltshire

For my gorgeous, talented, intelligent friends
eagerly awaiting a trip down the aisle.
I'm looking forward to a boogie after your bridal waltz!

CHAPTER ONE

DREAM dates were difficult to find. Eve Pemberton should know. She'd tried. Boy, had she tried.

With an exasperated sigh, she prodded at the gilt-edged, gold-embossed, ludicrously expensive wedding invitation propped in the middle of her desk.

It didn't budge, folded on its crisp columbine cardboard edges, immovable, rigid, taunting her with its stand-up stiffness.

She knew what she had to do.

She just didn't want to do it.

Taking a deep breath, she swept the invitation aside and flipped open her laptop. Now was as good a time as any to continue her quest to find her dream date.

'This is business,' she muttered, her fingers

flying over the familiar keys as she skimmed a few new search engines before finding what she was looking for.

Here goes nothing.

Squinting at the screen, covered in tacky ruby hearts, she stabbed at the enter key, hoping this wouldn't take too long. She had a million things on her to-do list today, starting with chasing recalcitrant subcontractors for one of the corporate marquees at the Australian Tennis Open to ensuring it was all systems go for an event kicking off the AFL season at the Melbourne Cricket Ground.

She loved her job as events coordinator and would much rather be scoping out Aussie Rules footballers than finding her dream date via a dating agency on the Internet but she had to do this.

She had no choice.

The first profile flickered to life on the screen and her tense shoulders relaxed a tad. Not bad. Nice face, nice smile, just…nice. Pity she didn't want nice. She wanted drop dead gorgeous.

While her fingers clattered and she viewed

close on twenty-five guys, her hopes sank. There wasn't a stand out among them, not the kind of guy she needed to impress *the bridal babes*—her friends Linda, Carol and Mattie—with. She'd been single at every wedding within their social circle for too long and she'd had enough. Throw in the hoo-ha associated with being a bridesmaid, the only unattached bridesmaid at each wedding, and she really needed to pull this off.

Though they never said anything, she'd caught their pitying glances, their frantic scanning of the guests for a suitable 'fix-up' at each wedding, or worse, the occasional 'accidental' introduction to a long-lost second cousin.

She may as well arrive at every matrimonial shindig with the words 'dateless desperado' tattooed on her forehead.

Not this time. Mattie, the last of her single friends to tie the knot, was always extra-sensitive to her moods and she'd be damned if she spoiled her friend's day, inadvertently, by turning up alone.

Just one last wedding to attend, one last bridesmaid dress fitting… The thought perked her up for a moment and she renewed her search with vigour, reluctant to admit defeat when the fiftieth bland profile blurred before her.

All these guys sounded the same: searching for friendship with a view to a relationship, likes walking on the beach, enjoys cosy dinners.

Well, she didn't need friendship or a relationship or any of that other stuff, thank you very much. She was an industrious businesswoman who needed a date, nothing more, nothing less. She used the Net all the time for work, so finding a date via this medium should've been a cinch, right?

She'd already been on five dates—five excruciatingly boring, painful, blah dates—and nothing. Not a dream date among the shoddy lot.

This was her last shot, the last online dating agency she hadn't tried and, right now, her chances weren't looking crash hot.

With a disgusted snort, she pushed back from her desk, rubbed the bridge of her nose, when a grainy photo in the corner of the news home page caught her eye.

She clicked on the icon to bring up the story,

her breath instantly catching as the photo sprang to life, filling half her screen with twinkling blue eyes, a charismatic smile and a cheeky dimple which lent the striking face a boyish charm.

She'd wanted drop dead gorgeous.

She'd got her wish.

Only problem was, Bryce Gibson knew exactly how hot he was and, worse, knew exactly how he affected her.

Determinedly ignoring the adorable dimple she remembered all too well, she speed-read the article.

'"New headhunted hotshot advertising exec arrives in Melbourne from Sydney…needs to prove himself…expecting big things…" yada, yada, yada…' she mumbled under her breath, finding her gaze unwittingly drawn to the picture again.

Oh, yeah, Bryce Gibson hadn't changed a bit. Still too confident, too charismatic, too…everything.

He'd had charm to burn, and she'd faked immunity. Until Tony's twenty-first, the night that had changed everything.

She stared at his picture, remembering her

brother's coming of age party, her coming of age night.

That night had been the catalyst for where she was today: new look, new confidence, new personality.

She should thank Bryce: for flirting, for teasing, for making her feel like a woman for the first time in her life. Or she should kick him for what came after. After that almost-kiss…

Either way, she'd love Mr Overconfident to see her now…

Eve sat bolt upright and snatched her hand off the mouse as if she'd been burned.

Oh, no.

Bad idea. A very bad idea.

You need a date. A 'sexiest guy on the planet' date. The type of date to show your friends you're fine, you *can* hook a hot guy; you just choose not to.

Yeah, but this is Bryce cool-McCool Gibson we're talking about. Remember him? The guy who teased me? Who turned on that legendary charm until I blushed? The guy who went out of his way to pay me attention when I didn't want it, then, when I did, froze me out?

Yeah, but that was then. This is now. Wouldn't you like to show him how far you've come? Where's your pride?

But he'll think I'm some kind of desperado, asking him out on a date. Or, worse, that I still like him. And, besides, using a dating agency was all about business. A no-frills, no-expectation date.

And your point is? Why can't Bryce be about business?

Telling her voice of reason to be quiet, Eve shook her head and glared at Bryce's picture.

He fitted her date criteria in every way: attractive, successful, charming, the type of guy to turn heads, the type of guy who would prove once and for all to her friends she could pull a date like him, she just chose not to because of her career.

Drumming her fingers on the desk, Eve knew she had no choice. The guys she'd dated so far were below par and this last dating agency's potentials were a no-go, while she had the perfect date staring her in the face.

Her belly trembled as her fingers inched towards the phone, barely touching the receiver before she snatched them back.

She couldn't do it.

No matter how far she'd come, she couldn't just pick up the phone and ask him to be her date.

It was ludicrous.

It was crazy.

And the longer she stared at those deep indigo eyes, those tempting lips, remembering how close they'd once been to hers, it was a foregone conclusion.

They'd shared a spark, a hint of something she'd never dreamed possible that special night and, while it may have ended badly, there was nothing like a trip down memory lane to give a girl a confidence injection.

She'd used what had happened as a catalyst and had reinvented herself after that night.

Wouldn't it be great to show him how far she'd come, a kind of *in your face, Gibson, this is what you missed out on?*

But it was more than that and therein lay the

problem. She may be wary but she'd be a fool to believe she'd be totally immune to him, even after eight years. Girls like her never fully got over guys like him.

No matter how many designer dresses or trendy haircuts or killer shoes she had, no matter how many events she presided over like a queen, no matter how many bookings she had for the next year, there was that small, insecure part of her that hoped he wouldn't take one look at her and walk, like he had at the end of that night.

Rules, she needed rules. Clear-cut, don't-mess-with-her-head rules. Rules that would give her heart a resounding whack if she contemplated, even for a second, anything other than using him as a stopgap date for the wedding functions.

Eve's French-manicured fingernails absent-mindedly tapped a stack of documents in front of her as she debated the wisdom of cold-calling a guy she'd once liked and asking him to be her date for a specified period of time.

Wisdom? More like insanity, but, as her gaze

drifted over the documents, all perfectly logical and precise, and back to Bryce's picture, she knew she could do this.

She was a successful businesswoman, used to following processes and procedures to the nth degree. And that was exactly what dating Bryce for the next month would be—a process to get what she wanted: her friends convinced she was okay and a stress-free wedding for Mattie.

She could do this.

Ignoring a zoo's worth of butterflies in her stomach, she focused on that taunting wedding invitation and reached for the phone with a shaky hand.

No time like the present to see if hotshot Bryce with his hypnotising eyes and magnetic smile would come to the party—literally.

'Nice view, huh?'

Bryce turned away from his office window towards his colleague Davin; the Melbourne cityscape was great, but decidedly less glamorous than the million dollar Sydney harbour views he'd given up when he'd taken on his new role here at Ballyhoo Advertising Agency.

No big deal; he'd cope without the view, considering the scope of this opportunity. Ballyhoo was big in the advertising world, real big, and he couldn't wait to get stuck into this new challenge.

'Not bad. Though I won't be spending much time staring out the window with all this to keep me busy.'

He gestured to the tower of manuals Human Resources had dumped on his desk, making a mental note to start sifting through them and prioritising ASAP. He needed a jump-start here, needed to stay one step ahead.

'Have you met with Sol yet?'

Bryce shook his head, dropped into his executive leather chair. 'He's in Auckland for the day, said we'd touch base when he got back.'

'Right.'

Davin propped himself on the desk, opened his mouth as if to say something before shutting it again.

'And?'

His uneasiness increased as Davin fiddled with the pen holder, didn't quite meet his eye.

'You know we're the number one ad agency in Melbourne, right?'

Oh, yeah, he knew. Solomon Perlman, CEO of Ballyhoo, had extolled the agency's virtues at length when he'd headhunted him for the position. He'd been blown away by the company's mission statement, reeled in by the lure of new challenges, and Sol had rammed home his offer with a salary package that would make the Prime Minister blink.

Working for a company as big as Ballyhoo would send his career into the stratosphere, something he'd worked towards for the last few years, something he deserved after the hard yards he'd put in.

'Yeah, Sol might've mentioned the "premier agency" thing a time or two. What's your point?'

Davin squirmed slightly, his expression shifting between furtive and ingratiating, setting his smarm radar on high alert.

'We're number one because Sol only goes for the big contracts. He won't tolerate anything less.'

'I already know all this.'

'Rumour has it you've been brought in as some kind of proposed shake-up. Sol knows the clients you courted in Sydney; he wants the same results here, pronto.'

'Takes months to build up contacts in this industry. Sol knows that.'

'Just telling you how it is. Sol expects results and he's not a patient man.'

'And you're telling me this because?'

The avaricious gleam in Davin's beady eyes told him exactly why his new colleague was acting so buddy-buddy before he said a word.

'We're on the same team now.'

So when he brought in the big bucks, Davin would bask in the glory too. He'd seen his type in Sydney, had worked alongside hangers-on, the slack employees only too eager to ride the coat-tails of a go-getter.

'Speaking of teams, a bunch of us are heading out for drinks tonight. You in?'

The last thing he felt like was socialising with guys like Davin but he needed to scope out his coworkers, get a feel for how things worked around here and the quickest way was over a beer.

'Sure.'

'We usually head around the corner to the Elephant and Wheelbarrow around six.'

'No worries.'

'Later.' Davin raised a hand as he sauntered out of the office, a smug grin on his podgy face.

Relaxing into his chair, Bryce linked fingers and stretched forwards, wishing he could dispel Davin's words as useless drivel. But he couldn't. Ballyhoo was top of the advertising heap and he'd just signed on as the newest executive. Sol would expect results, fast.

What if he couldn't deliver?

Doubt unfurled like a poisonous python, un-coiling, stretching and threatening to strangle his hard-fought confidence.

Failure didn't sit well with him. Never had.

Dropping his hands, he swivelled on his chair to stare out the window, hating the flicker of unease creeping through the deepest, darkest part of him—the doubting part, the part he'd conquered a long time ago with every successful deal he'd clinched.

The phone rang and he grabbed it, annoyed he'd let one iota of his old doubts creep in today, on what should be the start of another giant leap up the career ladder for him.

'Bryce Gibson speaking.'

'Bryce, it's Eve Pemberton. Tony's sister.'

He didn't need clarification. He knew who Eve Pemberton was. What he wanted to know was what she'd done to her voice. She'd never sounded this mellow as a teenager. Then again, she'd barely spoken back then. Until that night he'd rather forget.

'Hey, Eve, how are you? Long time, no hear.'

'I'm fine, thanks.'

She paused and his curiosity ratcheted up. What would mild-mannered Eve want with him, especially after how things had ended between them?

As if reading his thoughts, she hurried on. 'I have a business proposition for you. Are you free to meet me for a drink after work?'

'Actually, I'm busy…'

The words died on his lips as he caught the softest sigh on the other end of the line. If he didn't know better, he would say she sounded disappointed. Why? Apart from Tony, who he hadn't seen since he'd moved to New York eight years ago, they had nothing in common.

'The geek', some of the kids had called her behind her back, exactly why he'd gone out of his way to talk to her. He knew what it was like being the odd one out, even if he'd done his damnedest at the time to make sure nobody knew it.

'What about tomorrow?'

If he'd barely caught her disappointed sigh, there was no mistaking the hint of desperation audible in her dulcet tone.

Cool, quiet, aloof Eve Pemberton desperate? As if.

'Business proposition, huh?'

He deliberately lowered his voice, insinuating a different type of proposition, and almost laughed out loud at her sharp intake of breath.

Eve wasn't a woman he should flirt with. He'd tried it once; look how that had turned out.

'With you being new to Melbourne, it's in your best interests to meet with me.'

He opened his mouth to cite a prior engagement when she murmured, 'You won't be disappointed.'

He ricocheted upward so fast his knee clunked the overhang under his desk and he silently cursed while staring at the phone as if she'd reached through it and tweaked his ear.

The Eve he'd known had never sounded like that: soft, breathy, with an underlying hint of promise. Except the night of Tony's twenty-first, a night he'd deliberately erased from his memory, a night filled with promise, a night ended in shame.

Shaking his head, he pressed the phone to his ear, knowing he was crazy for hearing anything other than brisk politeness in her tone.

'Bryce?'

Making the type of snap decision he was famous for in the ad world, he double-checked his diary.

'I have to put in an appearance at a work function around six this evening. Maybe we can catch up later?'

'How about the Aria bar at the Langham Hotel? Around seven-thirty?'

'No worries.'

'Great. See you then.'

'How will I know you?'

He made a joke of it, wanting to end their weird conversation on a light note, wondering if he'd imagined the desperation.

'I'm sure you'll have no trouble recognising me.' Her tone, tremulous and uncertain as she hung up, left him staring at the phone in confusion.

Shaking his head, he punched the details into his BlackBerry. Eve Pemberton wanted to discuss business. But what business could they possibly have in common after all these years?

Come seven-thirty, he had every intention of finding out exactly what that was.

CHAPTER TWO

SHE'D lied.

Not only did Bryce have trouble recognising the lithe, leggy goddess walking into the swank Aria bar, he would've pegged her as someone other than Eve Pemberton by the confident toss of her highlighted hair swinging in a shiny dark chocolate curtain over her shoulders.

The Eve he knew had never been confident. She'd slunk around with shoulders slouched, huddled over a mountain of books, pushing her bottle-thick glasses up her nose while nibbling on the end of a pencil.

Gone were the glasses, as were the wide-leg jeans, baggy T-shirts and shapeless cardigans she'd worn like a compulsory uniform back then.

His gaze travelled the length of her, from the deep purple trouser suit the colour of ripe plums to the matching two-tone shoes. Designer, all of it. The kind of outfit that screamed success—and showed off a body he'd never imagined in his wildest teenage fantasies.

She scanned the room, her gaze locking on his as he smiled, waved her over, surprised by her answering grin. Genuine. Warm. Dazzling—the type of smile that made every man in the room turn his head to watch her wind her way between the tables.

'Bryce, good to see you.'

She held out her hand and he shook it reflexively, stung by the uncharacteristic urge to kiss her in greeting.

They weren't exactly strangers...not after the confidences they'd shared that night, the same confidences that had prompted him to act like a heel when his mates had laughed at their almost-kiss and he'd laughed along with them.

The memory shamed him and, with a mental slap to the head, he gestured for her to take a seat.

'You too. You look great, by the way.'

A tiny flicker of uncertainty flashed across her face before she sat down with a toss of her hair. 'Amazing what contacts and a new wardrobe can do for a girl, huh?'

It was more than that, much more. There was a self-belief about her, an inner poise that couldn't be faked or manufactured and her self-assurance had him intrigued.

What had happened over the last eight years to turn the shy girl he remembered into a sophisticated, elegant woman who apparently didn't have a qualm about calling him up and asking him to meet her after all this time, after that night?

'I would've recognised you anywhere.'

He smiled—the same smile he'd used to great effect over the years to woo clients and influence women—as he gestured a waiter over. 'Eight years isn't that long.'

Her eyebrows shot up in an *are you kidding me?* inverted comma.

'Still the charmer, I see.'

Leaning forward, he braced his elbows on his knees, staring straight into her deep brown eyes.

'Is it working?'

She laughed, a soft, sweet sound he'd heard many times the night of the party, when she'd responded to his witty banter rather than ignored him, as she usually had.

'I didn't come here to be charmed. Though some of that might come in handy for the deal I want to propose.'

'Deal?'

If her new persona hadn't intrigued him, the mention of a deal did. There was nothing he liked better than sealing deals.

The arrival of a waiter stalled their discussion and he sat back, resting his arm across the back of the chair, content to watch her turn the young guy into a red-faced fool with a nonchalant smile and a twirl of her hair around her finger as she placed an order for sparkling mineral water with a twist of lime.

Eve Pemberton, shy bookworm, had morphed into a chic woman. He'd been expecting standoffish Eve with average dress sense and aloof demeanour, not this…this…*babe!*

'Right, where were we?'

She turned back to him, her eyes glowing like warm molasses, and for a second he forgot the surprise of her call, forgot her fascinating deal, forgot the cringe-worthy finale at Tony's party, and wondered what it would be like to be sitting here on a date with her.

'The deal you mentioned?'

'That's right, the deal.'

Taking a gulp of his usual after-work caffeine hit, he tried to ignore the secretive smile playing about her mouth, the intriguing sparkle in her eyes.

He was an expert at reading non-verbal body cues, had mastered it from a young age to make up for his other shortfalls, and, if he was reading her correctly, this deal was more than business…

As if. Seeing her again, seeing her like this, had thrown him more than anticipated and his mind, used to creative flights of fantasy in devising innovative advertising pitches, was having fantasies of an entirely different nature.

'It's quite simple, really.'

She leaned forward, the smile fading as her eyes fixed his in a no-nonsense stare.

'I have a business proposition for you. One I think you'd be hard-pressed to pass up.'

'I'm listening.'

For the first time since he'd seen her, she appeared less than confident as she toyed with the serviette beside the drinks coaster. She picked it up, opened it, refolded it, pleated it before balling it into a crumpled mess and throwing it on the table and leaning back, hands clasped in her lap.

'I read that you're new in town, working at some top ad agency?'

He nodded, eager for her to cut to the chase. The faster they wrapped up this business stuff, the faster they could get onto more interesting topics, like what she'd been doing for the last eight years, who she'd been doing it with, was she still doing it with any significant others?

'Ballyhoo. The CEO made me an offer I couldn't refuse.'

'Congratulations. The article mentioned something about you chasing big contracts to prove yourself. Is that right?'

'It's the way the ad world works, yeah.'

Why he'd entered the field, why he kept working at being the best. He loved striving, loved proving himself over and over.

'Good. In that case, how would you like a personal introduction to some of Melbourne's biggest business names?'

'Great.'

What's the catch?

One of his first lessons in the business world had been—*if something sounds too good to be true, it usually is*—and this out of the blue phone call from Eve, combined with her suddenly false, brittle brightness, screamed that there was more to this.

'I just need one thing from you in return.'

'What's that?'

She paused, nibbled on her bottom lip, a strangely erotic movement that had him focusing on its fullness, its sheen, its teasing curve, remembering how close he'd come to kissing her, really kissing her, that night too long ago…

'I need you to be my date for a month.'

CHAPTER THREE

BRYCE'S eyes widened, his jaw sagged slightly. Not that Eve could blame him. It wouldn't be every day some desperate female in need of a quick date dressed up her ridiculous proposal in business terms.

He recovered quickly. Typical. Nothing had fazed young Bryce, the guy who'd swaggered around school halls as if he didn't have a care in the world and didn't give a damn what anyone thought of him.

He'd stood up to kids and teachers alike, famous for his wisecracks, cutting people down to size in the flick of an eraser. She'd avoided him for that very reason. Plagued by enough insecurity to keep Cinders scrubbing floors for a decade rather than attend a ball, she hadn't needed some cocky know-all turning his razor tongue onto her.

Not that he'd deigned to notice. If anything, he'd gone out of his way to chat to her. Nothing major, just small talk—small talk that came with a gorgeous smile and a twinkle in his startling blue eyes. Though only when he'd dropped around their house; at school, he was a year ahead and way too cool to acknowledge a dweeb like her.

She couldn't remember when she'd first developed a crush on him. Early teens? Later? But somewhere between Tony bringing him home for skateboarding and finishing high school, she'd looked forward to their brief encounters, even though she retreated inwards with every chat.

The more he noticed her, the further she withdrew, hiding behind aloofness because she didn't want him knowing what an insecure mess she was inside and how much she liked him. Besides, how could a guy like him consider noticing a girl like her—baggy clothes, glasses, a bookworm—as anything other than the sister of his best mate?

Tony's twenty-first had changed everything because she'd wanted to take the first fragile step towards acknowledging her femininity and what better way than testing out her meagre courage on the guy she'd secretly liked for years?

When he'd approached her out of politeness, she'd responded to him for the first time ever, blown away when he hadn't dumped a punch cup in her hand and headed back to the dance floor with a beautiful blonde on each arm.

Instead, he'd talked to her, flirted with her, feeding her teenage crush until it'd been inevitable they'd kiss.

Almost kiss. Big difference; yet another thing she'd regretted about that night.

These days, she didn't have time for regrets, which made her entrance ten minutes ago all the sweeter—when she'd seen him almost fall out of his chair when he'd first laid eyes on her.

'You want to *date* me?'

His lips kicked up at the corners and her wavering resolve dived for cover as she gripped her bag, ready to make a run for it. Her fingers dug through the leather to the stiff wedding invitation beneath, a none-too-subtle reminder of why she was here, humiliating herself like this.

Only one month. One month of wedding festivities before she could return her attention back to what she did best: business.

'No, I don't want to date you; I want you to be my date. There's a difference.'

She relaxed her death-grip on her bag, forced herself to relax. 'My last single friend is getting married and I need a date to accompany me.'

His smile broadened. 'Sounds easy enough. I'm flattered you asked—'

'Don't go getting any ideas. This will purely be a business arrangement. You accompany me to a few functions in exchange for introductions to the upper echelons of Melbourne's business world. That's it.'

It had to be. She wouldn't be foolish enough to think for one second that sexy, dimpled smile was anything other than a practised move known to charm, that the appreciative glow in his cobalt eyes was solely for her.

Bryce Gibson was mesmerising, always had been, and he'd had girls swooning from the time he'd put on his first pair of those ripped, frayed denim jeans he used to wear. If she'd thought he was cute as a kid, it was nothing on the magnificent male before her now.

He was one hundred per cent drool-worthy, from those playful eyes to those kissable lips, from his broad shoulders encased in crisp cream cotton to his long fingers caressing a very lucky coffee cup.

She'd wanted drop dead gorgeous to impress the bridal babes and Bryce would deliver. As long as she didn't go getting any crazy ideas—like how much fun it would be to date him for real.

She didn't date as a rule, found the whole process tedious at best, mortifying at worst. Guys were intimidated by her success or used her to get to the starlets she arranged functions for. She'd had three short-term relationships, if two months of dating apiece constituted a relationship. When casual verged on commitment, she quit. Not from some deep-seated phobia against long-term; she'd just never found the right guy.

So, rather than put herself out there, she preferred a quiet night in over making inane small talk with overconfident guys hell-bent on making a false impression.

Yet, with Mattie marrying, and her being the last bridesmaid standing, so to speak, she couldn't help but feel she was missing out on something, that being single and successful wasn't all it was cracked up to be.

Bryce sipped at his coffee—long, leisurely sips designed to make her wait, driving her anxiety levels sky-high—and she squirmed, wondering if she should've stuck to the Internet after all.

Staring at his picture on a screen was one thing, having those too-blue eyes focused unwaveringly on her another.

Laying his coffee cup on the table, he sat back and casually draped an arm across the back of his chair as if he were propositioned by crazy event managers every day of the week.

'Tell me more about these business contacts.'

This she could deal with: cold, hard facts. Facts to impress him, facts to woo him, for she had no doubt his business brain would jump at the chance to meet who she had in mind.

'You would've heard of Hot Pursuit?'

'Biggest sporting company in Australia?'

'That's the one.'

She paused for dramatic effect—completely unnecessary, for any ad exec worth their pitch would jump at the chance to meet AJ.

'I know Angus Kilbride quite well. He's the groom. So I'm guessing an intro to him at the pre-wedding dinner, a well-wish at the wedding, a casual beer or two at the post-wedding barbecue and a friendly hand of poker at the cocktail night video viewing mightn't be a bad thing?'

She snapped her fingers, throwing out the line a little further, ready to reel him in.

'My friend Linda is married to Anton Schultz, of the German Anton jewelers, and another friend Carol's husband is Duane Boag, of Australia's biggest real estate chain.'

She wouldn't have been surprised to see dollar signs light up his eyes but Bryce had class as well as looks for he fixed her with a steady stare, as if trying to ascertain her real motives, and she was the one forced to look away.

'Impressive contacts.'

He shrugged, a dismissive gesture that had her hopes for a dream date to dazzle the bridal babes with fading fast.

'I'll be honest with you; I could do with an introduction to businessmen of that calibre.'

'But?'

His gaze stabbed her, probing, questioning, demanding answers she had no intention of giving.

'I'm wondering why you've asked me. A woman like you would have her choice of dates. Why me?'

Especially after how things ended at Tony's party. The unsaid hung between them, as if he was prompting her to bring it up, get it out in the open. And she would, if he agreed to her deal. If not, she'd relegate the memory to the dim, dark recesses of her mind where she'd stored it as fuel for her new life.

Secretly thrilled he was deluded enough to think she could pull any guy she wanted, she shrugged.

'Would you believe it's fate?'

His eyebrow shot up in a perfectly inverted V as his mouth twitched. 'No.'

'It was. I was working online when I came across an article on you and when I heard you were new in town…'

She trailed off, hoping he'd buy her little white lie, aware he hadn't by the knowing glint in his eyes.

'You took pity on me. Yeah, I get it.'

His hint of bitterness surprised her but, before she could get a read on his mood, he chuckled. 'I'm also intrigued. And I could do with some new contacts, so it looks like you've got yourself a deal.'

'Great!'

Could she be any more pathetic? Being thankful he'd agreed to her dating deal was one thing, practically jumping out of her seat and pumping the air with a raised fist another.

'I still don't get why you had to approach me, though.'

She'd hoped he'd leave it alone. Now she'd have to give him some snippet of the truth.

'I'm a businesswoman, a busy one. I run my

own events management company so I socialise
for a living, day and night.'

She picked up the drink the waiter had de-
posited a moment earlier and took a sip. 'What
little down-time I get, I spend at home.
Basically, I don't have much spare time to
date.'

Or trade mindless small talk, pretend to be
interested in over-inflated egotistical ram-
blings or fend off the inevitable grope after
one drink, which most of the guys she'd dated
seemed to expect.

Give her a big kitchen, fresh ingredients and
the latest recipe book to hit the stands and she
was much happier. Though gourmet cooking
wouldn't show the bridal babes she wasn't a sad
case and, right now, the guy staring at her with
increasing intrigue in his eyes would.

Suddenly, an awful thought insinuated its way
into her head and she almost groaned aloud.

'I'm sorry. I didn't ask if you were seeing
someone.'

How stupid could she be? She'd been so caught

up in her plan to secure him as perfect date material she'd overlooked a very salient point: his availability.

He wiggled his ring-free left hand in front of her.

'No attachments here. No wife, no girlfriend.'

Leaning forward, he crooked his finger at her, leaving her little option but to shuffle forward on her seat, ending up way too close to him.

This close, she could see the sea-green flecks in his eyes, the faintest end-of-day stubble prickling his cheeks and the sexy groove bracketing his mouth on the right.

She'd always had a thing for dimples, could almost reach out and touch it. Trace it. Dip a fingertip in it…

'I'll let you in on a little secret. I wouldn't have agreed to date you if I was seeing someone. What kind of guy do you think I am?'

His conspiratorial wink merely added to his roguish charm and she inhaled sharply, needing some air to clear her fogged head. The tantalising scent of freshly brewed coffee and crisp citrus filled her senses, making her want to reach out, haul him closer and bury her nose in his chest.

'On second thoughts, don't answer that.'

He laughed and sat back, breaking the intimate spell and she clamped her lips together to stop herself from reneging on the daft deal right this very minute.

'So how's Tony? I haven't heard from him in years.'

'He's fine. Taking Wall Street by storm.'

'Still in merchant banking?'

She nodded, wishing her only family didn't live half a world away.

'Yeah, he hasn't been back to Australia in years. I'm surprised you two didn't keep in contact.'

'Guys tend to drift apart. We started moving in different circles after high school.'

But he'd been at Tony's twenty-first, so they hadn't lost contact totally.

That night was imprinted on her brain. She'd felt gauche and awkward and out of place in her new formal dress, the only dress she owned, a bright blue stiff taffeta that had made odd crinkly noises when she'd moved, while Bryce had swaggered into the party wearing a cocky grin as if he owned the place.

And he had. He'd been the life of the party, had talked and laughed his way through the first hour while she'd stayed in the shadows like a wall-flower, wishing a guy like him would notice a girl like her.

As if by some inexplicable, intangible force, her wish had come true. He'd spied her on the outskirts of the room, edging towards the balcony of the trendy Albert Park club Tony had hired for the party, and followed her.

For the next hour they'd talked, laughed, ribbed, and she'd come alive under his attention. She'd never felt that way before, had been stunned that a few minor changes in her appear-ance—contact lenses, new dress, lipstick, high-heeled shoes—could give her the power to flirt with a guy like Bryce.

Even after what had happened later, she'd never forgotten that feeling, how good she'd felt, had been desperate to reproduce it. She had—

reinventing herself after that night, hadn't looked back.

And wouldn't start now, not with Bryce staring at her, that dimple only a lip quirk away.

'Last time I saw him was at his twenty-first.' His gaze flicked over her suit, leaving a trail of tiny goose bumps as if he'd touched her. 'You too, remember?'

Oh, yeah, she remembered every tiny detail, from the faded denim jeans he'd worn to the tan bomber jacket he'd slung around her shoulders when she'd shivered, more from his attention and proximity than the cold.

She remembered him handing her a champagne, the touch of his fingers brushing hers giving her more of a buzz than the bubbles sliding down her throat.

She remembered leaning on the balcony railing, gazing out at the stunning view, lights reflecting in the shimmering surface of Albert Park Lake with Melbourne's city skyline in the background, with him standing behind her, close behind her, his body spooning hers, until he'd held her arms, turned her around and…

She blinked in a desperate attempt to obliterate the memory of what came next, knowing they had to acknowledge the unspoken but not wanting to discuss it now.

His lips curved into a sexy smile as he reached out, placed a finger under her chin and gently tipped it up.

'We need to talk about what happened that night.'

She couldn't move, couldn't look away, trapped in the heat of his stare, her skin prickling beneath his fingertip.

This wasn't good, this…this…*awareness*. How could she keep things strictly platonic between them if she reacted like a schoolgirl with a giant crush on the high school jock the second he turned his charm on her?

And he would, of that she had no doubt. Charm was as natural to Bryce as breathing and it meant nothing. She'd watched him exercise it at will as a teenager, had seen girls literally lean against walls with weak knees as he'd strutted past.

Not her. Uh-uh, no way.

She'd been smarter than that, had hidden her

reaction behind coolness; that did little to stop him. She'd been a brainiac, could never explain her aberrant reaction to a guy with a glib line and a flirtatious dimple he used as a weapon. Until she realised something. Not everything had a logical explanation and, with a guy like Bryce, her reaction had been instinctive, hormonal, visceral.

Not any more. Please, Lord, not any more.

Forcing a laugh, she ducked her head and glanced at her watch. 'As much as I'd like to stay and reminisce about old times, I've got work to do.'

'Right,' he drawled, leaving her in little doubt he didn't buy her lousy excuse to escape. 'How about we schedule another time to catch up?'

'Catch up?'

His smile widened, as if he knew exactly how flustered he made her.

'If you want your friends to think I'm dating you, surely we need to get together before the first function and get our stories straight? Practise acting lovey-dovey, that sort of thing?'

Practise acting lovey-dovey…

Heck, what had she got herself into?

Her horrified expression must've clearly shown her trepidation for he laughed and squeezed her hand. 'Relax, I'm kidding. But we do need to chat because we're going to get asked the basics like how we met, was it love at first sight, all that kind of stuff.'

'You're right.'

She'd intended to set up a meeting to do just that, until he'd befuddled her senses with his potent presence.

'Can I give you a call? I'm kind of swamped with a few events at the moment.'

'No worries.'

He laid a steadying hand under her elbow as she stood and, with his innocuous touch sending sparks shooting through her body, she knew it was easy for him to say.

No worries, indeed.

CHAPTER FOUR

BRYCE tried to focus on Sol droning on about profit margins but his mind kept drifting back to his meeting with Eve.

He'd been over it in his mind countless times, replaying everything she'd said, every nuance, every expression and he still didn't get it. Sure, he'd bought her story about not having time to date and wanting this to be just business but that was where his confusion kicked in. She'd said she socialised for a living, would know loads of guys on a platonic basis, so why hadn't she asked any of them to be her date?

And why him, especially with how things had ended at the party? She couldn't even talk about it, yet had proposed a convenient arrangement, one he'd been more than happy to accept, considering her terms. While Eve may be singing the dating deal tune, he knew there was more to it. And he had every intention of finding out what that was.

'Bryce? Where are you at with new clients?'

Wrenching his attention back to the meeting, he withdrew several meticulous lists from his portfolio. His colleagues in Sydney had labelled him the 'list king' and it had stuck. Not that he cared. He'd always worked that way, found lists helped him organise and prioritise and focus, keeping him at the top of his game, right where he wanted to be.

'I've made a list of contacts I'm in the process of following up.'

Sol narrowed his beady eyes, probing, assessing. 'Who?'

'Angus Kilbride. Anton Schultz. Duane Boag. For starters.'

'Impressive list.'

Sol rubbed his chin, one of several, before pinning Davin with an intimidating glare. 'Isn't there a rumour the Hot Pursuit contract is up for grabs soon?'

Davin's head bobbed so furiously it was a wonder it didn't fall off. 'No rumour; it's fact. One of the major players on their last campaign just quit and hasn't been too circumspect with information.'

A shot of adrenalin pumped through Bryce's veins. Man, was he glad he'd agreed to Eve's deal. Not only would he get an informal intro to Angus, he might have inside running to nail the lucrative contract.

'Right.' Sol's gaze swivelled back to him, calculating and predatory. 'If Kilbride is on your hit list, make sure you secure the Hot Pursuit contract.'

'Got it.'

And he would. Failure wasn't an option, not here, not now, not ever.

Sol's steely gaze lingered on him a tad longer, as if trying to size him up before sweeping over the rest of the conference table. 'As for the rest of you, I want to see results by next week.'

He thumped the table while Bryce smothered a smile. He was used to the theatrics of the ad world. He'd worked with the best, had seen some shows in his time with keen up-and-comers trying to secure big campaigns.

Personally, he'd rather let his work do the talking, the creative ideas that flowed like a steady stream when he took on a new project, something he never doubted and thanked the big guy upstairs for every day.

'I want each of you to bring a new client to the table this time next week. Bryce, you get a month because you're new in town and aiming high. That's it. Get to work, people.'

A month? He'd landed bigger fish in Sydney in a fortnight. But who knew, maybe things worked differently in Melbourne? Maybe the networking circles were harder to break in to? Which was exactly where Eve came in and the thought of pretending to be her date made him do an inner high-five. All that hand-holding, cuddling, maybe a kiss or two for authenticity's sake…

'You really think you can land Hot Pursuit?'

Shoving documents into his folder, Bryce stood and gave Davin a perfunctory nod.

'I wouldn't have said it otherwise.'

The calculating gleam never left Davin's eyes for a second. 'If you need a hand, don't hesitate to ask.'

The day he asked the toady for help was the day he'd admit defeat: never.

'I'll keep that in mind.'

Sending a pointed glance at his watch, he picked up his paraphernalia, gave Davin a casual wave and headed for the door. Now the meeting had wrapped up, he had another to attend. One that would prove a lot more fun.

Eve slid her hand into a potholder and lifted the lid, inhaling deeply as the delicious aroma of slow-cooked Moroccan lamb filled the air in a burst of cinnamon fragrant steam.

Humming to herself, she sprinkled a generous handful of torn coriander over the top and turned the stove to low, letting the dish simmer before replacing the lid.

She shouldn't have gone to all this trouble but she'd been nervous and, when she was nervous, she cooked. Other people worked out, went for long walks or meditated. She cooked.

She'd cooked her way through high school.

She'd cooked her way through her dad's death when she was eighteen.

And she'd cooked up a veritable feast the minute Bryce had said he'd be dropping around tonight so they could go over their dating story.

Cooking was therapeutic. Cooking was relaxing. But, as she stared around the kitchen, noting the fluffy couscous with preserved lemon, the roasted vegetable pilaf and the Mediterranean stack of chargrilled eggplant, zucchini and Roma tomatoes, she knew there'd been little unwinding and loads of stress involved in the culinary masterpieces she'd concocted.

She reached for her wine glass, took a healthy sip, too wound up to savour the divine Clare Valley Shiraz.

He'd be here any moment. The guy she was supposed to be dating, the guy who had to convince her friends she wasn't a desperate singleton.

One more bridesmaid stint, one more wedding—one more teensy-weensy wedding—before the last of the bridal babes were married off and she wouldn't have to fake the whole *I'm cool and successful and happy being single* at another ceremony.

She was happy being single most of the time, but there was something about this wedding, something about Mattie joining her other friends in matrimonial smugness that grated.

The slight condescension that came with being part of a happy couple wasn't intentional—the girls would never do that to her—but being surrounded by it had worn thin. The constant touching and eye-contact and in-jokes were fabulous—if you were the one involved in the relationship.

And while she loved hanging out with her best friends and their men, the constant pressure of being the only unattached female in blissful coupledom left her feeling like a third wheel most of the time—and somewhat miserable, if she was completely honest.

Hopefully, turning up with Bryce in tow would give her a legit excuse to beg off a few gatherings after the wedding rice settled.

Once she'd survived the next month and all

the wedding events, she could return to doing what she did best: work. And unwinding on her terms, in her place, without the expectations of socialising with the aim to find a partner.

She couldn't rely on people. She'd learned that the hard way. Her business, her home was steady, dependable and she liked it fine.

A sharp knock sounded at the front door and she gulped the rest of the Shiraz in record time, shooting a last frantic glance at her reflection in the oven door before smoothing her hands over her favourite beaded top and heading down the hallway at a deliberately slow pace when in fact she felt like bolting—in the opposite direction.

With a deep breath, she opened the door, sending Bryce the confident smile she'd spent weeks practising when she'd first opened Soirée. With Bryce staring at her as if she were a gorgeous goddess, it was all worth it.

'These are for you.'

He handed her a bunch of beautiful gerberas in tangerine, buttercup and garnet. No standard issue carnations or clichéd roses for Mr Tall,

Dark and Charming. Uh-uh—when he wanted to impress a girl, he went all out.

'Thanks, but you didn't need to.'

With a slow conspiratorial wink, he stepped over the threshold.

'Ah, but I did. I'm getting into practice for my role as your date.'

Disappointment filtered through her before she gave her conscience a swift, sharp kick. She wanted him to do this right. So why the momentary lapse in reason, the split second where she'd wished he'd brought her flowers just because he wanted to, because she was deserving of them?

'Good idea; come through.'

She marched up the hallway, instantly regretting her rather brisk response. Where were some of those deportment skills when she needed them?

'Something smells great.'

'Hope you're hungry,' she said, smiling at the irony of the statement.

She could've catered one of Soirée's premier events at the Town Hall with the amount of food she'd cooked, let alone feed one hungry charmer. Entering the kitchen, she made for the stove, knowing the exact moment he followed her into the room.

'What the…'

Turning around, she laughed at his stunned expression and beckoned him to take a seat at the island bench dominating the room.

'Are we expecting company?'

She shook her head, picked up a wooden spoon and gave the tagine a last minute stir before switching off the stove.

'I like to cook. It's my relaxation.'

'Gourmet, by the looks of it.'

He picked up one of the crudités and dunked it into her special smoked salmon and Camembert dip before popping it into his mouth, his satisfied expression soothing her chef's heart.

She liked cooking but she also liked seeing people enjoy food and, by the look of sheer bliss on Bryce's handsome face, he was really enjoying it. Imagine how he'd look during other activities he really enjoyed…with a shaky hand, she filled a wine glass for him, refilled hers.

'This is great.'

'Try these too.'

She shoved a platter of tiny samosas and curry puffs under his nose, pleased when he popped three into his mouth in rapid succession, happy to feed him the entire contents of the counter if it kept them from talking.

Crazy, considering they needed to get their story straight if Linda, Carol and Mattie were going to believe this was real but, having him here, in her home, had rattled her more than she'd anticipated.

Her home was her sanctuary, the one place she could shut out the world and be herself. Her confidence mask slipped off the minute she removed the contacts from her eyes and wiped off the day's immaculate make-up, her posture relaxing the instant she shrugged out of her designer suit and donned her oldest frayed jeans and tatty T-shirt.

She'd spent years building a professional persona to hide the insecure girl she'd once been but, the moment she stepped through her front door, she slipped into her old skin, more comfortable than ever.

Picking up her wine glass, she gestured to the backyard. 'Do you want to sit outside for a while or are you starving?'

Patting his stomach, he wrinkled his nose. 'After the number of those tasty treats I just demolished, let's sit for a while.'

Eve knew she should respond, should put one foot in front of the other and head for the door, but she couldn't think, couldn't move, for the second he patted his stomach her gaze had riveted to his jet-black polo shirt and the way it highlighted flat, to-die-for abs.

She could see the faintest ripple of muscle, the delineation of the fabled six-pack and her mouth watered, having little to do with the heady aromatic spices of the tagine and everything to do with his great body.

'You've changed.'

His soft words lingered in the air and she wrenched her gaze up to meet his, recognising a flicker of desire which mirrored her own.

'Guess I'm not a geek any more, huh?'

He visibly started before quickly masking his shock with a rueful smile. 'Kids can be cruel.'

Oh, yeah, she knew that first-hand. Her less than cool clothes, her thick glasses and her IQ hadn't exactly endeared her to her classmates back in high school. Then again, she hadn't really cared. She'd never had the confidence to match it with the cool girls, or the sporty ones for that matter. The only time she'd cared was on the odd occasion when Tony had brought Bryce home…and he'd been a balm, treating her as if she wasn't a dork, making her fall a little bit in love with him every time for noticing her, let alone talking to her.

She picked up her wine and headed for the back door.

'I was a geek. The kids just called it as they saw it.'

He followed her, his stare boring into her back and sending heat flushing through her.

'I never called you that.'

'What I could never figure out was why.'

She pushed the door, held it open for him. With a puzzled glance he stepped through, grabbing her arm when she made to move past him.

'I know you don't want to talk about this, but we have to,' he murmured, his long, strong fingers hot on her skin, his equally hot gaze lighting an instant fire between them.

'What happened that night is irrelevant.'

'I don't think so.'

Giving her arm a gentle squeeze, he dropped his hand.

'I was an idiot that night.'

Something dark, almost painful, shifted in his eyes, at odds with the cocky, brash kid who'd commanded attention without trying, at odds with the confident, powerful man he was today and, for a guy who wore his self-assurance like an aura, the hint of vulnerability was beyond appealing.

'Not for all of it.'

'When it counted most.'

His compelling stare locked on her, imploring her to remember. She needed little reminding as her gaze dropped to his lips, remembering the exact moment their entire evening had gone pear-shaped—the second before his lips had touched hers.

'Don't beat yourself up. So we almost kissed? And your mates saw us. They teased you; you said it meant nothing.'

She gave him a little shove towards her patio table. 'You were right; it didn't. Now, take a seat and I'll bring out the hors d'oeuvres.'

By the determined glint in his eyes, he wanted to labour the point, to discuss how she'd down-played what had happened, but she was through playing the reminiscing game. If she was going to get through the next month, she needed to focus on now, not the past and the embarrassing crush she'd had on a guy out of her league.

'Eve, it wasn't like that—'

'Back in a sec.'

Desperate for time to reassemble her wits after he'd shot them down in a conflagration of flames with that innocuous touch on her arm, she fled.

Bryce let Eve go, despite the urge to…what?

Get her to acknowledge what a jerk he'd been

that night? Get her fired up so he copped some well-deserved anger? Get her to admit most of that night had been amazing until he'd screwed up?

What was he going to do—badger the woman in her own house?

From the stack of cookbooks piled in higgledy-piggledy disarray in the cosy kitchen to the sprawling English cottage garden filled with wild flowers spread before him, he could see she invested time in her home.

She'd always been a homebody, had filled her childhood home with vases of violets, had done most of the cooking for her dad and Tony. Their mum had died when they were toddlers and, while Tony had never spoken about it, he wondered if that was the reason behind Eve's nurturing side, her urge to create a home beyond a simple house.

Not having a mum must've been tough on her, especially as a teenager, when she hadn't fitted in. He'd seen the hurt in her eyes when she admitted knowing about the geek nickname, had felt it like a kick in the guts and, while he'd never called her that, he'd thought it.

He'd almost blurted out the truth right then and there—anything to wipe that pain away—but what good would it do? He was here to act as her impressive date, not give her reasons to doubt him.

The screen door creaked open as she backed through it, arms laden. He leaped up to help, but not before he let his appreciative gaze linger on her fine butt, clad in denim, her funky top riding up as she elbowed the door, giving him a tantalising glimpse of tanned skin above her waistband.

She'd always been lean, athletic, but this new and mature Eve had filled out in all the right places, lending her a softer feminine edge—an edge that had him itching to run his hands all over her.

'Let me help you.'

'Thanks.'

She handed him a platter filled with vol-au-vents, smiled her thanks—a small, shy smile at odds with the confident, go get 'em woman she'd been when they'd met at the bar.

He admired the successful businesswoman she'd become—doing a Google search had clued him in to exactly how successful she was—yet found this homely version as appealing.

He, who only dated models and soap actresses and 'It' girls, who hadn't had a home-cooked meal in for ever, who didn't like houses for the very fact they screamed to be filled with noisy kids and the entire family kit and caboodle, was attracted to a woman so obviously connected to her home? The cleaner Melbourne air must be getting to him.

Pulling out her chair and scoring a dubious look for his trouble—he had to remember that; she wasn't used to chivalrous guys—he sat opposite.

'Apparently our past's off-limits; let's talk about our deal. How do you want to play this dating thing? Do you want your friends to know we used to hang out or am I the new love of your life?'

Her stare could've withered the violets on the table between them, though the corners of her mouth twitched.

'We never used to hang out, though I think we ought to pretty much stick to the truth.'

'Which is? That I'm your new main man and you can't keep your hands off me?'

Grinning, he popped several crudités into his mouth, enjoying the faint blush staining her cheeks. Oh, yeah, he loved this susceptible side to her, the soft core of the confident city girl.

'Speaking of which...' Her blush deepened and she bolted down half of her wine before continuing. 'We might have to hold hands, drape an arm around waists, that sort of thing to make it look authentic. Hope you don't mind.'

Mind? Was she kidding? The first opportunity he got, he'd be sliding an arm around her waist and cuddling her close. If she was this delightfully flustered just talking about it, he couldn't wait to see how she'd react when they did it for real. He might've mucked up royally the night of Tony's party, he'd be damned if he made the same mistake twice.

Biting on the inside of his cheek to keep himself from chuckling, he mustered his best guileless expression.

'What about kissing?'

'No kissing.'

She stuffed a samosa into her mouth, chewed

frantically, masticating the thing to mush in less than a second.

'Couples kiss all the time. It might add to the authenticity of your plan. You want them to believe we're dating for real, don't you?'

She muttered something that sounded decidedly unladylike before sending him a slightly tremulous smile which had him wanting to leap over the table and haul her into his arms. She was adorable, every contrasting inch of her, and going through with this crazy dating scheme was going to be more fun than he'd thought.

'Let's just take it as it comes, okay?'

Keeping the victorious grin off his face, he nodded before reaching across the table and taking hold of her hand, his pulse picking up tempo as her tongue darted out to moisten her bottom lip.

'You don't have to worry. I'm going to be the model date.'

By the flicker of doubt in her expressive chocolate-brown eyes, that was exactly what she was afraid of.

CHAPTER FIVE

EVE had known that inviting Bryce into her home would be a bad idea but she'd gone ahead and done it anyway.

Madness, when every move she made in the business world was calculated to the nth degree. She hadn't turned Soirée into Melbourne's number one events management company without some sound decisions, including changing her image. She'd hired a wardrobe consultant, make-over artist, hairstylist to the stars, even done a stint at a deportment school to improve her posture, to project the image she wanted—that of a poised, confident business-woman at the top of her game.

She'd handled huge events with aplomb, mingled with the upper echelons of Melbourne society, prided herself on cool, methodical decisions. So what was with the fuzzy brain syndrome ever since she'd approached him to be her dream date?

Watching him fork the last of her pistachio panna cotta with honey syrup into his mouth, a satisfied sigh escaping his lips as an expression of sheer bliss spread across his handsome face, she had her answer.

Staring into those indigo eyes, seeing that groove flash in and out of his right cheek at will, those lips curved in a permanent smile, what chance did a girl have to think straight?

Patting his stomach—she wouldn't look, she wouldn't look, oops, there she went, catching a quick peek—he groaned, an all too sexy sound as he pushed back from the table.

'That was categorically the best meal I have ever had.'

Thrilled by his praise, she pushed her own plate away, surprisingly relaxed considering they hadn't nutted out the dating logistics yet.

'I find that hard to believe, considering hotshot

ad execs like you would be wining and dining clients in five star establishments all the time.'

His eyes crinkled adorably when he smiled. 'And, like I said, this is still the best meal I've ever had.'

'So let me get this straight. A simple lamb tagine with baby carrots, a bit of couscous and a super-sweet dessert does it for you?'

The instant the words left her mouth she knew she'd said the wrong thing, for his eyes darkened to midnight, the resident cheeky glint replaced by something more seductive.

'You have no idea what does it for me,' he murmured, searching her face for—what? Agreement? As if he'd get any argument from her! 'But I guess, as my date for the next month, you're about to find out.'

Oh, boy.

She began gathering up crockery at record speed, unprepared for his hand to snake across the table and still her forearm.

'Leave them. After a meal like that, the least I can do is clear away and wash the dishes.'

Her skin burned beneath his palm, hot, fierce, as a sizzle of sensation zinged up her arm, jolting her into realising she'd better lay down some firm ground rules for their dating quick-smart before her haywire hormones had other ideas of what dating Mr Charming entailed.

'Okay. But don't wash them. Just give them a quick rinse and stack the dishwasher. I'll turn it on later.'

Oh-oh. Poor choice of words again and she quickly slid her arm out from under his hand, needing to establish some physical distance between them.

With her mind in a tizz, her body joined the party in a big way, popping champagne corks and flinging streamers and stringing up a banner bearing the message, *Surprise! Eve Pemberton still has a monster crush on Bryce Gibson.*

'Sit tight; I'll be back in a minute.'

Watching him gather plates, stacking them with the cutlery on top, she couldn't help but notice his strong forearms dusted in a smattering of dark hair, his long, almost elegant fingers and the sure way he handled her precious crockery.

Her gaze drifted upwards; his polo shirt pulled taut across his broad shoulders as he leaned across the table, his biceps flexing deliciously while he piled his arms high.

Mmm…definite benefits to having him clear up and as she tried, and failed, to not look over her shoulder as he strode through her back door, a little sigh of longing escaped her lips.

Bryce Gibson was seriously gorgeous.

Not just in a physical sense; the time they'd spent together tonight had proved she'd mis-judged him all those years earlier.

Maybe he'd been trying to fit into the cool crowd, maybe he'd had issues she didn't know about, maybe he'd just been growing into his own skin, as most young guys did, but the man she'd pinned as a jerk at the conclusion of Tony's party was nothing but charming and lovely and utterly irresistible.

'Must be some mighty nice thoughts to put that smile on your face.'

Lost in her musings, she started as he slid into the chair opposite. 'You don't want to know.'

Unable to do anything but return his disarming smile, she wondered why he made her feel so inept. It wasn't as if she'd never handled flirtatious guys before. She met all types in her work, socialised with people from all walks of life, from mega-wealthy CEOs to office gofers. Yet Bryce could undermine her with a flash of his even white teeth beneath the curve of those sensual lips.

He interlocked his fingers, stretched them behind his head. 'Oh, I get it. You were thinking about how I'm going to be a great date.'

She tried to quash the bubble of laughter at his mock smugness and failed, chuckling when he pretended to check himself out.

'Not that I blame you. I'm pretty irresistible.'

Considering he'd just echoed her very thoughts, he'd get no arguments from her. But she couldn't let him know how he still affected her, how much she really liked him, how much she wished they were dating for real, and the sooner they discussed specifics about their dating the sooner she could bundle him out of the door and try to vanquish images of enigmatic blue eyes and deep dimples.

'Modest too. Let's talk about the upcoming functions before I lose my head completely in your overwhelming masculine presence.'

'Are you making fun of me?'

She held up her thumb and forefinger about an inch apart. 'Just a little?'

His eyes twinkled with delight as he reached across and closed his fingers over hers, sending her into instant meltdown. Heat raced up her arm, swift, scorching, warming her better than the spicy lamb she'd served.

So much for vanquishing. She needed to get this briefing done ASAP before the cravings of her body overrode her sensibilities.

'Teasing is good,' he murmured, his tone low and husky, undoing her as much as his sexy smile. 'Teasing is what dating couples do, so nothing like getting in a little practice.'

Yeah, right, practice. That was what she'd been doing. Not.

'Exactly.'

Sliding her hand out from his on the pretext of taking a drink of water, she ended up guzzling the entire glass in several unladylike gulps, desperate to douse the flames burning her up from the inside out.

This was sooo not going to work, this *let's keep our relationship platonic while you pretend to be my date; it's all business* plan she'd concocted.

But she couldn't back out now. She'd already had Mattie on the phone this afternoon, subtly suggesting she buddy up with a third or fourth cousin removed at the wedding rehearsal dinner, so she'd done the only thing possible and blurted out the truth about Bryce.

Well, an adulterated version of the truth: that she'd met someone, they were dating and he'd be accompanying her to all the wedding functions.

Mattie had oohed and aahed, and Eve knew she would've barely made it off the phone before her enthusiastic friend had conference-called Linda and Carol to give them the goss. Both girls had rung her mobile a scant half hour later and she'd let the calls go through to messages, too busy working out her stress in the kitchen at the time.

She'd been wound up enough about Bryce's imminent arrival without having the bridal babes tag-teaming her with their special brand of, *Is he the one? Is he gorgeous? Is he rich? How long before you're walking up the aisle and having his babies?*

She loved her friends but, boy, did they have one-track minds when it came to weddings and the fabled happily-ever-after—hence the nickname she'd given them years ago.

'Top up?'

He held the ceramic water pitcher out to her and she shook her head, eager to get this evening back on track.

'No, thanks. I'd really like to chat about our arrangement.'

'Okay, then, down to business.'

He whipped a notepad and pen from his pocket, scribbled a few headings and drew up columns.

'You're taking notes?'

'I want to make sure I get the details correct.'

The tightening around his mouth eased as he

pointed at his notepad with the pen. 'You want to convince your friends, right? Well, I need to make sure I remember the little things and it pays to put in the hard work.'

She couldn't fault him for that ethos, so why the niggle of doubt that there was more to it?

'You've mentioned the functions I have to attend; how about you give me a little background on your friends?'

'Mattie is the bride. She's a flight attendant, which is how she met AJ.'

'Angus Kilbride is AJ?'

'Angus James Kilbride. Everyone calls him AJ.'

Bryce raised an eyebrow, as if questioning the informality of calling Australia's biggest sporting empire mogul by his initials as he scribbled notes.

'Right. What about your other friends?'

'Carol's married to Duane Boag, who you've heard of. Biggest chain of real estate agencies in the country. And Linda's hubby is Anton Schultz, the jewel king. She's a publicist, Carol's a copywriter. The babes are the best.'

'Babes?'

His other eyebrow shot up to join the first and she laughed. 'I call them the bridal babes. Ever since Linda first walked up the aisle, they've been obsessed with weddings. I've been a bridesmaid at each of their weddings and, thankfully, this one is the last.'

She waited for him to trot out the trite 'always a bridesmaid, never a bride', grateful when he didn't.

'You didn't mention you were a bridesmaid.'

'Foregone conclusion with the bridal babes. No one in our circle is released from duties such as trying on hideous satin dresses, enduring hair trials with Edward Scissorhands and getting buffed and spray-tanned to within an inch of our lives.'

He grimaced. 'Sounds painful.'

'You don't know the half of it!'

They laughed. 'So, if they're obsessed with weddings, does that extend to getting you partnered off?'

She nodded, instantly remembering embarrassing 'coincidental' meetings with *suitable friends* at Linda's infamous dinner parties, Carol begging her to accompany her to work functions, only to discover a desperate and dateless colleague she *had* to meet, and Mattie setting her up on a blind date with a pilot who'd yawned through the entire evening—short-lived as it had been.

And she wasn't even thinking about the parties where some poor unsuspecting single guy would be foisted on her or both weddings, where she'd been shoved towards a lone best man or groomsman.

'They just don't seem to get it, the fact I'm happy with my job and don't need some guy to complete my life.'

With a playful wink, his lips curved into that oh-so-sexy smile that turned her insides to mush. 'So that's why you haven't just picked *some guy* to impress them; you picked me.'

Chuckling at his teasing, she waggled a finger in front of him. 'Don't go getting an inflated ego. You just happened to pop up on my computer screen at the right moment.'

'You were looking for a date on the Net?'

Battling a surge of embarrassment guaranteed to heat her cheeks, she nodded.

'I thought it'd be quick and easy. Log onto a dating site with all those guys at my fingertips and choose one. I use the Net for business every day so it should've been a cinch.'

'So what happened?'

You, was what she wanted to say.

You, with your incredible blue eyes and your cute dimple and your smile that could melt a nun at a hundred paces.

You, with your broad shoulders and sensational abs and charisma that practically oozed through the PC screen and was so much more potent in reality.

Instead, she chose her answer with care.

'Honestly? I'd been on a few dates and nada. The guys on those dating sites all sound the same, like they'd rehearsed answers to get chosen.'

His lips twitched. 'Let me guess. Walks on the beach. Cosy dinners. Weekends at B&Bs in the countryside.'

'How did you—'

'I did a campaign for one of the biggest sites in Sydney. My research was thorough.'

'Sure was.'

They laughed, their easy-going camaraderie reminiscent of the past and that one fabulous night where she'd captured his attention for an all-too-brief moment in time.

Eight years was a long time and she hadn't expected to like him this much. She'd thought they'd get the ground rules of this dating arrangement established, make a bit of polite small talk and that was it. No way had she expected to be blindsided by his charm, struck by his natural warmth and friendliness all over again.

Bryce was something else. The bridal babes would be blown away—her intention all along.

But what if she was blown away too?

What then?

CHAPTER SIX

POISE.

Plan.

Precision.

The words she'd once read in some self-help tome reverberated through Eve's head as she stood in front of her wardrobe, her hand uselessly trailing along the season- and colour-coordinated clothes.

To be poised for the rehearsal dinner and her grand entrance with Bryce, she needed a plan—a solid plan to follow with precision.

So far, her plan to wow Bryce and boost her confidence with a fabulous dress had hit a snag—a big one.

She didn't own the type of dress she needed.

A va-va-va-voom dress, a knockout dress, a dress that would make a guy like Bryce unable to tear his eyes off a girl like her.

That dress wasn't in her closet. She should know; she'd been through every single one of her expensive designer dresses: all very sleek and elegant and lovely, but not a hint of va-va-va-voom in sight.

With a disappointed sigh, she unhooked a hanger and held her newest little black dress at arm's length. Knee-length, fitted, V-neck, its cut clung and flattered in all the right places.

But it wasn't a knockout and she thrust it back into the wardrobe and slammed the door, glancing at her watch and groaning as she realised it was too late to make a dash down Chapel Street before the boutiques closed.

It was at times like this she missed having a mum. She'd never had someone to help her choose clothes or do her hair or show her how to apply make-up, had been envious of the other girls in her class when they'd rolled up to the school gates with their yummy mummies dressed in fashionable clothes and

dazzling smiles and bestowing hugs on reluctant daughters.

She would've given anything to have that kind
of relationship but her mum had died when she
was too young to remember and, while her dad
had done his best, she often wondered if she
would've been more outgoing, more confident if
she'd had a woman's advice.

In her teens, while girls her age were dressing
in hip denim and experimenting with make-up,
she'd been at home experimenting with fresh
herbs and recipes. Not that she'd ever begrudged
cooking meals or housekeeping for her dad and
Tony, but every time she'd seen a classmate stroll
through the school gates in the latest wedges
with mascara-enhanced eyelashes, a small part
of her had really wished she had a mum.

Staring daggers at her uncooperative wardrobe,
she turned away, her gaze lighting on her open
laptop where she'd been doing a bit of work
earlier.

'You dolt,' she muttered, plopping onto the bed
on her tummy and yanking the laptop close, her

fingers flying over the keyboard as she Googled several chic Australian designers and came up with a plethora of online boutiques.

If she'd found the perfect man online, she should've known finding the perfect dress there would be the obvious place to look.

A tingle of excitement grew exponentially as she scanned the various sites, seeing some killer dresses but not *the one*. Until her eyes landed on a new up-and-coming designer with an unpronounceable name and she jolted upright, slapping her hand over her eyes, too scared to look in case the picture she'd seen was a figment of her wishful imagination.

Spreading her fingers a centimetre apart, she peeked through, letting out an excited squeal as she saw it.

The dress.

With enough va-va-va-voom to make an entire male revue cast take notice.

Clapping her hands in glee, she leapt off the bed, did a little shimmy before darting a glance at the price, not particularly caring how much it cost. She worked hard; she deserved to own the most heavenly dress on the planet.

Even on the computer screen the dress shimmered and danced, its bold silver sparkling, catching her eye and making her yearn to run her hands over the gleaming fabric.

She had to have it.

Plonking down on the bed, her fingers shook as she placed the order, express delivery.

Come tomorrow, she'd have the dress.

Come tomorrow night, she'd have the man.

Since when did her life get so exciting?

'No last minute pep talk before I wow your friends?'

Sending Bryce a tremulous smile that hid a wealth of nerves, she said, 'Glad to see you're not short on confidence.'

He patted her hand tucked under his elbow and winked.

'With a gorgeous woman on my arm, you bet I'm confident.'

Slipping into routine, assuming a role, that was

all he was doing, yet with his smouldering gaze skimming her body and his touch doing crazy things to her insides, she almost believed him.

'So we're straight on our stories? How we met, that sort of thing, how—'

'Relax.'

He brushed her cheek with the back of his knuckles, a soft, barely-there caress that sent her belly into freefall and her limited bravado with it.

Relax? Was the guy insane? How could any woman relax with someone as sexy and suave and sophisticated staring at her as if she was his girlfriend for real?

Relax, indeed.

'Come on, the faster we get in there, the faster you'll relax.'

Not on your life, she thought as he held her hand, intertwining their fingers in such a way that felt way too comfortable, way too right. They shouldn't fit like this and tonight shouldn't feel like a real date.

But it did. And had, ever since she'd slipped into the Silver Streak, her knockout dress. The dress was beyond va-va-va-voom—way beyond—and the second Bryce had first laid eyes on her and his jaw had sagged she'd known it was worth every cent.

He'd recovered quickly, the shock in his eyes replaced by something much more potent, much scarier as he'd started at the top and worked his way down, his hungry gaze devouring her.

Her skin tingled at the memory and her grip inadvertently tightened, wishing she could back out of this ludicrous plan now, knowing it was too late.

'You're having second thoughts.'

It wasn't a question, and the fact he could read her mind so easily, could sense her unease, had her more worried than his hand holding hers.

'Am I crazy doing this?'

He smiled, and the power behind that one simple action slugged her all the way down to her toes.

'You're a professional businesswoman who doesn't have time to date. There's no shame in being single.'

He tipped up her chin and she gulped, hoping he couldn't read the rush of anticipation his touch elicited. They were so close—close enough for him to duck his head and…

'But if you want to show up with a date for all the wedding tribulation, I'm all yours.'

If his caress on her cheek a few moments ago had unnerved her, his thumb brushing her bottom lip almost undid her completely.

Bryce Gibson was all hers, even if it was only for a month. Why the heck was she hesitating?

Hoping a toss of her hair would distract him from her wobbly knees as she swayed towards him, she nodded.

'Let's do this.'

'That's my girl.'

With a squeeze of her hand, they climbed the few steps and pushed through a giant glass door, pausing at the entrance of The Anchorage.

Butterflies alternated between tap-dancing and slam-dancing against the walls of her belly as she took a deep breath—several—only a matter of time until one of her friends caught sight of her.

A sudden hush fell over the intimate restaurant

and she could've sworn she heard a collective indrawn breath as Mattie caught sight of her, followed by Linda and Carol in quick succession, courtesy of several sharp elbow jabs in the ribs from the bride-to-be.

'We've been spotted.'

Bryce's broad grin screamed he loved every minute of the unfolding drama as he ducked his head to whisper in her ear, 'Do you want me to kiss you now for an extra convincing touch?'

'No!'

His low chuckle broke the tension, his twinkling eyes with the endearing creases going a long way to soothe her nerves. Not a moment too soon as the bridal babes wound their way through the tables, making a beeline straight for them.

'Show-time.'

Sliding an arm around her waist, Bryce sent her friends a charismatic smile as they descended into bedlam.

'Hey, hon, you look fabulous.' To Mattie's credit, she managed to mouth 'wow' at her dress before her curious gaze zeroed in on

Bryce. 'And you must be Eve's new man. Pleased to meet you.'

Refraining from rolling her eyes as Linda and Carol elbowed each other out of the way for next in line introduction honours, Bryce handled her crazy friends with aplomb.

With an encouraging squeeze of her waist, he dropped his hand to shake Mattie's. 'Bryce Gibson. Pleased to meet you.'

Making room so Linda and Carol could squeeze in, he said, 'So which of you lovely ladies is the blushing bride?'

They all twittered like excited birds presented with a juicy worm as Eve silently applauded. She had to hand it to him; rather than being put off by her friends' whirlwind introductions and non-stop chatter, he was in his element, bestowing smiles and winks and charming compliments.

Thrilled he was living up to his end of the bargain, she slipped a hand into his, hating how good it felt, loving the dimpled smile he bestowed on her.

'Meet Mattie, Linda and Carol.' She waved to

each of them in turn before doing a theatrical hand flourish back at him. 'Girls, Bryce.'

'Charmed, I'm sure.' Carol's casual once-over started at Bryce's hand-made Italian leather shoes, ended at his twinkling blue eyes and encompassed everything in between as she gave her a thumbs up sign of approval behind her back.

'Great to meet you, Bryce.' Linda's effusive greeting and wicked grin matched Carol in the subtlety stakes and Eve stifled a groan as Mattie slid a possessive hand through his other elbow.

'Come and meet the guys while we interrogate our friend.'

Squeezing her hand for reassurance, his lips curved into a sexy grin that kick-started her stalling heart as he allowed Mattie to lead him away. 'Be gentle with me.'

Mattie chuckled. 'No promises.'

'Girlfriend, we have got to talk,' Carol muttered under her breath as she and Linda propelled her to follow.

'You have some serious explaining to do, young lady!'

* * *

Eve's best innocent look was lost on Mattie as her friend all but dragged her into the swanky Ladies' room while the rehearsal dinner was in full swing. Linda and Carol were already waiting on the plush persimmon velvet chaise longues in the cosy foyer, none too patiently by the way they jumped to their feet as soon as they entered.

'Eve! Oh, my God, where did you find that man? He is absolutely gorgeous!' Linda gushed, grabbing her arm and tugging her towards a chaise longue while Carol all but shoved her down with a 'He is a total hottie! Tell all!'

Laughing, she held up her hands. 'Can you girls give me a minute here?'

She shrugged off their clinging hands and smoothed down her silver sheath with deliberate slowness, knowing it would drive the inquisitive trio barmy.

'Eve Pemberton, if you don't tell us right this very minute what's going on, I'm afraid we'll be forced to take drastic action.'

Mattie stood over her, hands on hips, her Titian ponytail bristling like a sunburnt hedgehog.

She knew better than to cross the babes in full inquisition mode and she held up her hands in surrender.

'Okay, okay, just let me catch my breath.'

She paused for effect and exhaled slowly. 'Trying to keep up with Bryce has me exhausted.'

'You mean—'

'Have you two already—'

'You go, girl!'

Laughing, she crossed her legs at the ankles, admiring her sky-high silver stilettos. She'd caught Bryce checking them out, though he hadn't stopped there.

In fact, when she'd opened the door to him a few hours earlier, he'd taken a good long look at her clingy dress and sparkly shoes before holding out his hand to her, twirling her around and murmuring a soft, sweet, 'You look absolutely stunning.'

Coming from him, she felt stunning and in that magical instant he'd obliterated the awful memory of him leaving her alone on that balcony, her skin pebbling with cold, her face flushed in mortification, as he'd rejoined his friends, who were laughing at her.

She'd never worn anything like the Silver Streak, had never had the confidence to wear something so fitted, so glittery. But tonight demanded it and, if Bryce's gobsmacked expression and hungry gaze had been any indication, her confidence boost had worked.

The Eve he'd once known—ugly duckling— had transformed into the proverbial elegant swan. While she still felt the same on the inside—uncertain, confused and bamboozled by his attention— it was great to gain the admiration as an attractive woman she'd once hungered for from him.

Not that she was trying to prove a point. They'd moved past that the moment she'd walked into the Aria and seen the genuine male appreciation in his heated blue-eyed stare.

Uh-uh, this was about her—all about her. She'd spent an inordinate amount of time over the years building her image, shedding her old look, building a confident outer shell to the world that no one could breach. She never went out in public without full make-up, contact lenses and stylish clothes.

The babes, her three closest friends in the world, teased her about it. Then again, she'd never seen any of them look anything other than immaculate, stylish and chic. Crazy, but they were friends from her 'new' life and a small part of the old her, insecure, craving approval, wondered if they'd still like her if they saw the real her. The Eve that Bryce knew.

He was the only one who'd seen her back then, apart from Tony, who loved her as a sibling regardless. And the old Bryce had walked away from her without a backward glance.

Which brought her full circle to the dress…and ensuring he saw how far she'd come, how little his rejection meant.

Rolling her eyes, she pushed off the chaise longue and headed for the mirror, lipstick at the ready. 'Relax, ladies. We've only been dating a short time. We're still getting to know each other.'

'Oh.'

The babes sighed in disappointed unison and she shook her head, chuckling at their morose expressions.

'Cheer up, girls. I'll be sure to let you know when anything juicy happens.'

Yeah, right. Not that she hoped anything remotely report-worthy would happen…right?

Mattie fanned her face and plopped onto the chaise longue. 'With a guy like Bryce, juicy is only a matter of time. Phew, is he hot or what!'

Surprised by the niggle of jealousy at her gorgeous red-headed friend finding Bryce attractive, and more surprised by the tiny flicker of hope at what juicy with him might entail, she played it down.

'I thought you girls might be impressed.'

'Impressed?' Carol smoothed her sleek bob as if the man in question had just entered the room. 'Eve, honey, that man is beyond impressive.'

'Hear, hear,' Linda chirped up, her resident cheeky smile alerting the rest of them she was about to drop one of her classics. 'I recently read an article comparing guys' sex appeal to chocolate and, in Bryce's case, he's the finest Swiss ever invented.'

Bryce…chocolate…yum…

As three sets of curious eyes swung her way, Eve briefly wondered if she'd said that last bit out loud.

As she rejoined them on the chaise, Mattie laughed and patted her arm. 'That expression on your face says it all.'

She had an *expression?* She couldn't, not when this dating thing with Bryce was strictly platonic.

Uh-uh, no way would she be silly enough to read more into it, just because he'd stroked her arm, held her hand and casually touched her every chance he'd got tonight. They'd discussed it, remember? Small physical displays of intimacy would be expected from a dating couple if she wanted to convince the girls.

Carol and Linda smirked and headed for the mirror for a quick make-up repair job. 'Come on, leave the girl alone. Can't you see she's so gaga over the guy she can't wait to get back out there?'

'I'm not gaga,' Eve said, desperately ignoring the sinking feeling that maybe she was.

Bryce was in his element.

Great party, great food, interesting people, sparkling conversation—and a stunning woman by his side.

Eve chose that moment to enter the room and his gaze zeroed in on her, his gut instantly tightening with longing as he watched her sashay between the tables towards him.

She was something else.

He'd dated models and soap opera starlets, women as uninterested in commitment as he was, but none of them held a candle to this beautiful woman. It was so much more than appearance. Her quiet confidence, her subtle class combined with a killer brain had him wanting to get to know his faux date a lot better.

Reaching his side, her glossed lips curved in a tentative smile—a smile that tugged on his heartstrings, a smile that insisted he sweep her into his arms and show her exactly how gorgeous she was with a kiss to end all kisses.

But it wasn't the time or place. Or was it?

She wanted to convince her friends they were dating; what better way than to…?

'Whatever you're thinking, get it out of your mind right now,' she said, the flare of heat in her eyes making a mockery of her words.

'Where's the fun in that?'

He whipped out her chair, placing a hand in the small of her back to guide her down, not surprised by the slight stiffening.

Eve may have made it clear she didn't want anything from this dating deal beyond what they'd agreed but her body didn't lie and right now it was begging him to put their platonic agreement to the test.

'The girls are very impressed.'

'With me?'

'No, with my new BlackBerry.' She rolled her eyes as he laughed. 'What do you think?'

'I think I'm going to have a lot of fun convincing your friends we're a couple.'

'You've already done a good job so far.'

'Bet I can do better.'

He ran a finger down her bare arm, lingering in the hollow at her elbow, savouring her sharp intake of breath as he continued downward to caress her pulse point, the frantic beating a clear indication he was having the same effect on her as she was on him.

'I think you've done enough.'

Her voice sounded shaky but she didn't move away and, emboldened by her nearness, her intoxicating vanilla fragrance so reminiscent of the delicious dessert she'd concocted the other night and the heat simmering between them, he slid an arm around her waist and pulled her flush against him.

'Not nearly enough,' he murmured as his gaze locked on hers, daring her to stop him, hoping like hell she wouldn't.

'This isn't part of the deal—'

He kissed her, driven by an all-consuming need to discover how she responded to him as a man, how she felt in his arms, how she tasted.

He'd aimed for a gentle testing kiss, an affectionate kiss between a couple just getting to know each other. However, when she angled her head ever so slightly and parted her lips on a small satisfied sigh, he lost it.

Completely.

Everyone, everything faded into oblivion as she came alive in his arms, kissing him back with a surprising hunger that fired him, inspired him and showed him what he'd missed out on all those years ago by foolishly walking away from her.

'I've wanted to do this since I first laid eyes on you tonight,' he whispered as he momentarily broke the kiss, hating his misplaced chivalry that demanded he give her time to pull back, wanting her more now than ever.

To his amazement, she touched her lips to his again, tentatively at first, before demanding a response he was only too willing to give.

Sliding his hand into her hair, he cradled her head while deepening the kiss to the point of losing control, losing his mind, losing sight of the real reason he was here.

Business. Where failure wasn't an option. And

being the platonic date Eve wanted for the duration of the month was paramount to success at his new job.

So what the hell was he doing taking a chance like this?

Breaking the kiss, he pulled away to look into her eyes, expecting censure, indignation, even anger.

The unguarded yearning glittering in the expressive dark depths had him reassessing the situation in an instant. If Eve wasn't mad about the kiss, if she looked like she wanted more, maybe he had a chance of making the next month more pleasurable than anticipated?

Why couldn't they date for real? Have a little fun, considering they both knew the score—that it wouldn't lead to anything, apart from what they both wanted out of it?

'Eve?'

'Hmm?'

'Did I just score a ten out of ten in the convincing stakes?'

'Don't know about them but I'm convinced.'

Her soft tone bordered on wistful as she raised

a hand to her mouth, skimming her fingertips over her lips while a dazed half smile played there, a smile that had him hankering to do it all over again.

'So am I.'

Unable to stop himself, he leaned forward and brushed a lingering kiss across her lips again, a kiss that promised more.

'You're good at this acting thing.'

Her blunt words doused him more effectively than if she'd flung her chilled wine in his face.

She thought he'd kissed her as part of the charade they were perpetuating. While it might've been his original plan when they'd first discussed this crazy deal, his intentions had changed along the way. Kissing her had nothing to do with proving a point to anyone and everything to do with the vibrant woman gnawing on her bottom lip and staring at him with confusion in her eyes.

He should leave it alone, let her go on thinking this was all part of the deal they'd figured out. That was the easy way, the uncomplicated way. Then again, since when had he ever done easy?

Sliding his hand into hers, intertwining their fingers, he said softly, 'What if I wasn't acting?'

Her eyes widened in shock, huge and dark and mesmerising, her teeth leaving off worrying her bottom lip only to be replaced by the tip of her tongue darting out to moisten it.

'B-but our plan—'

'Plans change.'

He tightened his grip on her hand, his thumb tracing slow, lazy circles on the back of it.

'They evolve. They grow. They develop into new and exciting possibilities.'

She didn't look convinced and, just as he expected her to yank her hand out of his, she smiled, a sunny radiant smile that warmed his heart better than the flush of success after his first promotion.

'You're good, Bryce Gibson, very good. I'm still not convinced at your motivation behind that kiss but I'll let you off this time.'

'With a warning?' He grinned right back at her, hoping she'd flirt with him and not retreat back into her cool, elegant shell.

Shaking her head, she said, '*You* should come with a warning.'

'And what would that be?'

'Dangerous goods, handle with care!'

He laughed, wondering how far he could push her. 'Come on, admit it.'

'Admit what?'

Her smile slipped as he focused on her mouth, on her deliciously plump, thoroughly-kissed lips, staggered by how badly he wanted to do it again.

'How much you enjoyed it.'

Folding her arms, she tilted her nose in the air like every disapproving teacher he'd ever back-chatted. 'I'll do no such thing.'

She even sounded like them, all prim and proper and stern, which only served to egg him on.

'I won't let up until you do.'

Sliding an arm across the back of her chair, he deliberately let his fingers ripple across her skin in the barest of caresses, vindicated by the slight shudder beneath his fingertips as she stiffened.

Ducking his head, he nuzzled the tender skin

behind her ear. 'I've got all night to keep this up and, believe me, I'm just getting started.'

'All right, fine, I enjoyed it. Satisfied?'

Her rigid back and hands-off posture would've been enough of a signal to have him backing down, if it weren't for the momentary fear he glimpsed in her eyes.

She wouldn't be scared if that kiss hadn't affected her as much as it had affected him and it gave him hope.

'A few more of those incredible kisses and I might be well on the way.'

'Oh, for Pete's sake.'

Her mock exasperation was blown when the corners of her mouth twitched and he chuckled, his arm sliding off the chair to rest on her shoulders, hugging her gently, bringing the side of her sensational body into luscious contact with his own.

'You enjoyed it as much as I did.'

She laughed, placed both palms flat against his chest and pushed lightly.

'Anyone ever tell you you've got confidence and then some?'

'In my job, it pays to be confident. Guess it's become a part of who I am.'

Damn, where had that come from? Curiosity shifted in her eyes but, thankfully, she didn't push him for answers he wasn't ready to give.

'Speaking of your job, how did you go with AJ? Any male bonding yet?'

He reached for his beer, grateful the heavy moment had evaporated quicker than his job if he didn't deliver what the boss man Sol wanted.

'He seems like a nice bloke. Duane and Anton too.'

Strangely, work had been the furthest thing on his mind since they'd arrived at the rehearsal dinner. He'd been focused one hundred per cent on Eve, all too aware of her long tanned legs stretched out beneath the table next to his, by the way the tight shimmery dress ended an inch above her knees, how it clung to her body and outlined every delicious inch.

He'd hung on her every word, had flirted and laughed with her, had concentrated on her and her alone, his plans for networking coming a distant second to ensuring she had a good time on their first date.

'They're all great, even though I had to face an inquisition of mammoth proportions from the bridal babes when I went to refresh my lippie.'

'They wanted to know about me, huh?'

She nodded, her lips curving in a playful smile. 'Every single detail.'

'What is it with women and the baring soul thing?'

Her smile faded, a wary expression darkening her eyes to the richest bittersweet chocolate.

'We look out for each other.'

He knew in an instant she was feeling guilty at deceiving her friends. He could see it in her down-turned mouth, in her tense shoulders, in her expressive eyes.

Squeezing her hand, he said, 'If you're worrying about us being here together, about you and me dating, don't. We're old buddies hanging out together for a while and I don't know about you but I'm having a great time. We'll stay in touch after all this is done, so don't

feel bad. It doesn't have to be any more complicated than that.'

Okay, so he'd stretched the truth a tad. They'd
never been buddies, far from it, but he wanted
to make her feel better, to bring back the lively
sparkle she'd had all evening.

Thankfully, she relaxed enough to lean into
him and murmur in his ear, 'Thanks for that.
You're a good guy.'

'Just good?'

Sending her an exaggerated wink, he raised
his glass in her direction.

'To being the best dating buddies.'

'I'll drink to that.'

If only he could focus on the buddy part and
forget how much he'd like to move on to being
so much more.

CHAPTER SEVEN

LYING to her friends didn't sit well with Eve.

They'd been genuinely excited for her at the wedding rehearsal dinner and it wasn't until later, when she'd been casually chatting with Bryce, did the depth of her deception hit her.

These girls cared about her; they wanted her to be happy. Yet in their eyes she needed a man for that. A theory she usually scoffed at but, with Bryce sending her into a tizz every time he glanced her way, she couldn't help but wish for that fabled happily-ever-after her friends were so good at touting.

Great, she was starting to believe her own hype. This plan was crazy but she'd have to perpetuate the deception a tad longer, go through with it until after the wedding, and when she'd shucked her bridesmaid dress for the last time she'd tell them the truth.

Which was what, exactly?

Groaning, she flipped open her laptop and brought up her diary for the day. Better to focus on work and forget how complicated the situation with Bryce was.

The guy was too irresistible for his own good. She'd wanted drop dead gorgeous to impress her friends; little did she expect she'd be the one equally impressed!

If dinner at her place had opened up a world of possibilities between them, pretending to be his girlfriend at the rehearsal dinner had been sheer and utter torture.

He'd been attentive, charming and utterly captivating all night. She'd barely noticed the divine oven-roasted duckling on a confit of new potatoes with five-spiced peach chutney and the mouth-watering apple and macademia crumbled tart drizzled with hot caramel sauce—her, the queen of gourmet cooking!

She'd paid scant attention to her friends, who'd

thoughtfully given her space to…what? Stare into Bryce's blazing blue eyes all evening? Chat with him like old friends? Flirt outrageously like she'd never flirted in her entire life?

As for those kisses…she squeezed her eyes shut but nothing could erase the memory of how he'd made her feel—like a desirable woman, a woman who could attract a guy like him.

It had been the dress, of course. He'd never seen her like that, had responded by slipping into a role he was an expert at playing: charming, flirtatious, gallant, a master at making a woman feel special.

It had been great while it lasted but she was under no illusions. If Bryce had seen her later—contacts out, make-up off, faded grey cotton pyjamas—he would've run, just like he had years ago.

Okay, maybe a tad unfair, as she hadn't been wearing anything remotely interesting the night of Tony's party, the peacock blue taffeta formal dress a reject from the eighties and, while she'd loved it, being the first dress she'd ever bought, she'd seen the aghast glances from fashion-conscious bimbos wearing slinky LBDs.

He'd seemed just as interested in talking to her that night, had made her believe for an all-too-brief time that he actually liked her for her brains, that appearances weren't important.

Until his friends had intervened and he'd acted like a loser. Now, like then, Bryce could turn. Once their deal was over, what if he reverted to ignoring her, pretending that none of this had happened? Wouldn't be the first time.

One kiss, and already things were getting way more complicated than anticipated. And if she felt this torn after one kiss, how the heck would she hold up until the end of the month?

Better to assume the kiss meant nothing, that Bryce had been playing the role assigned to him. She'd assumed he was performing but there'd been something in his tone, something in his eyes when he'd asked her, *'What if I wasn't acting?'*

Her heart had stopped when he'd said that, her over-sensitised body ready to jump him on the spot. Being the scaredy-cat she was, she'd laughed it off but he'd gone on to complicate matters by talking about things developing and growing and goodness knew what.

While *developing* something out of dating Bryce sounded appealing, she couldn't do it. She knew better than anyone how becoming too attached to someone could end.

Uh-uh, she wasn't cut out for the dating game, let alone a relationship, no matter how much she secretly craved it.

A knock sounded at the door and she opened it, ushering one of the AFL's marketing managers into her office.

The Australian Football League, a major customer, had helped propel Soirée to the top of events management in Melbourne, but as the slick guy droned on about his requirements for the upcoming Grand Final Ball she found her mind constantly wandering: to the way Bryce had filled out his suit at that first meeting at the Aria, the way he'd cleaned up the dishes at her house, the way he'd kissed her senseless at the dinner.

She managed to nod and smile and sound articulate with the client, saying all the right things

like how she'd theme the ball, include special
effects, organise the entertainment, devise a
suitable food and beverage package and organise
everything from invitation design to VIP con-
cierge service, but all the while she couldn't
forget the way Bryce's lips had felt moving
against hers, how he'd been tender yet passionate, skilful yet reverent, as if expecting her to
rebuff him.

As if. The moment he'd kissed her she'd forgotten every sane reason why they shouldn't be
doing it and had instantly been transported out
of this world—to a planet where ugly ducklings
really did end up with the prince.

Okay, so she was seriously mixing her meta-
phors but the memory of that one kiss brought
a goofy smile to her face every time she
thought about it.

'Any venues in mind, Miss Pemberton?'

Annoyed she'd been daydreaming when she
never let anything interfere with her profession-
alism, she handed the client a filled brochure.

'I love using unique locations so whatever you

want I can do. For other functions I've taken over disused warehouses, showgrounds, forts, passenger terminals, trains, swimming baths, building rooftops, quarries, islands, you name it, anywhere that's special I can arrange an event there to be remembered.'

The client, a dead ringer for a young Mel Gibson—did she have Gibsons on the mind or what!—appeared suitably impressed and she went with a decisive conclusion to her pitch.

'Just so you know, I don't rely on traditional props or well-worn themes. I like to come up with exciting, innovative ideas, the kind of tailored package you won't find with any other event company.'

Mel's double sent her a long penetrating stare before holding out his hand as he stood.

'I need to take this back to my marketing team but I can't see a problem. Looks like you've got yourself an AFL gala to coordinate, Miss Pemberton.'

'Thanks. You won't be disappointed.'

Shaking hands, she escorted him to the door,

leaning against it and exhaling in relief after he'd left.

She'd done it. Added another celebrated event to Soirée's impressive portfolio, the type of event that would bring mega-exposure.

When she'd landed big events previously she'd usually rush home, cook up a storm involving loads of quality coverture chocolate and lashings of cream, and listen to her favourite soul CDs as she curled up on the couch and savoured her victory.

So why the insane urge to pick up the phone, ring Bryce and share her good news with him? Or, worse, go out for a celebratory drink? Her, the antisocial queen out of work hours?

Madness. Pure and utter madness. Dating Bryce was about convincing the girls she wasn't desperate and dateless, that was it. No getting involved, no developing fanciful ideas about what it would be like to date the gorgeous Bryce for real.

Her wavering gaze drifted to the phone perched on her desk at a jaunty angle, taunting her, and her palm itched to cross the room, pick it up and dial.

No, she couldn't. She wouldn't.

The mobile in her pocket sang out its jingle at that precise moment and she sighed in relief, answering it without checking caller ID.

'How's my fabulous date today?'

Clenching the phone to her ear, she couldn't control the surge of sheer joy sweeping through her at the sound of Bryce's deep voice.

'Fine. Just thinking about you, actually.'

Cringing, she slapped the side of her head with her free hand. What was she thinking, telling him that?

The rumble of low laughter washed over her, rich and warm and oh-so-sexy, telling her exactly why she'd said that. She couldn't think when she heard his dulcet tones, let alone formulate a coherent, witty response.

'All good things, I hope.'

'I was thinking about work stuff.'

'Sure you were.'

His teasing tone brought a blush to her cheeks as she alternated between silently cursing him for reading her mind and cringing with embarrassment because he knew how much she liked him.

'Speaking of work, AJ contacted me and invited me to a product launch for Hot Pursuit.'

'Great.'

She was pleased for him. If she got what she wanted out of this dating deal, it would be good for him to get something out of it too.

'He suggested I bring my girlfriend. It's a partner thing too so Charlie's Angels are going to be there, along with buyers.'

'Charlie's Angels?'

He chuckled, a low, seductive sound that raised the hairs on her nape and sent heat flooding to places that hadn't been flooded in a long, long time.

'My nickname for your friends. What with Linda being blonde, Carol brunette and Mattie a redhead, it kind of fit.'

Joining in his laughter, she crossed the room on shaky legs—drat the man and his effect on her, even via the phone—and plopped onto her comfy ergonomic chair. 'Bridal babes, Charlie's Angels, wonder what the girls would think if we let them in on our little secret.'

'Which one?'

Not willing to acknowledge her guilt at not telling her friends the truth yet, not now, when she was on a high after her latest coup, she brought up her diary with a few clicks of the keyboard, thrilled when she realised her last client of the day had cancelled.

'Talking about secrets, how would my secret date like to come out and have a celebratory drink with me? I've just scored a major event.'

'Congratulations. A drink sounds great. Where and when?'

Wrinkling her nose at the stack of contractor invoices piled neatly on her desk, she said, 'How about I wrap up things here, which should take an hour, then I'll text you the details?'

'Sounds good.'

He paused as she heard the murmur of voices in the background, impatient voices by the sound of it, before he came back on the line.

'Sorry about that. New boss expects results like yesterday. So you'll come with me to the Hot Pursuit gig, yeah?'

'Sure.'

She had no choice. The girls would think there was a problem between her and Bryce if he showed up and she didn't.

'Good. Better get going. Chaos here. Looking forward to that drink.'

'Me too. Bye.'

She rang off quickly, eyeing the stack of invoices. The sooner she dealt with them, the sooner she got to let her hair down with Bryce.

As long as that was all she let down around him, for she had a distinct feeling if she let her guard down there'd be no recovering from it.

Eve smiled her thanks at the doorman as he opened the door to Bryce's apartment and waited until she entered before leaving.

This felt wrong, entering his apartment when he wasn't there, but he'd insisted and, rather than spending another forty-five minutes at the bar where they'd initially arranged to meet, she'd agreed to wait for him here.

Stepping into the lofty open-plan room serving

as lounge, dining and entertaining area, her mouth fell open as she took in the black sheer drapes framing the floor-to-ceiling windows and the giant chandelier hanging from an ornate ceiling, the leopard-print furniture, the black marble floors and the eclectic mix of candelabras, African animal figurines and coloured glass bottles.

A few dimmed down lights reflected off the ebony marble floors, shimmering like an oil slick beneath her feet while Melbourne's city skyline glittered through the sheer black chiffon like jewels scattered against an ermine cape.

The overall effect was surreal, sophisticated and decadent. A bit like the man himself, the man she'd first glimpsed in that photo accompanying the article online: suave, confident, a guy on top of his game, a guy ready to take on the world and win.

Bryce's apartment was very James Bond while her home in a quiet South Yarra street channelled *Little House on the Prairie,* from its green and cream chequered sofas to its soft-honey oak polished boards, its antique fireplace to the lemon walls.

The two places were worlds apart.

Standing in his apartment reinforced what she'd always thought, always known: they were two very different people.

She'd been kidding herself.

All his tender gazes, gentle hand-holding and intimate smiles had fooled her temporarily, his desirability blinding her to the facts.

Fact: Bryce was a charming, irresistible extrovert who could wend his way into the heart of any unsuspecting female, while she was an introspective introvert who faked confidence on a daily basis for her job.

Fact: Bryce was fun-loving and spontaneous and enjoyed partying, while she shed her cool image the second she walked in her front door and curled up on the couch with a book rather than go to a bar.

Fact: Bryce was her opposite in every way and, while he might be dating her to further his own ends, there wasn't the remotest chance he'd develop feelings for her.

The type of feelings she knew deep down were

already starting to blossom in her guarded heart, feelings she'd harboured as a teenager but dismissed as a crush, feelings that had flared to life the night of Tony's party, only to be doused by Bryce's cavalier attitude at the end.

Could she be any more pathetic? She'd been the one raving on about keeping their dating strictly platonic, about sticking to business and furthering their agendas.

Ha, ha, looked like the laughs were on her.

She'd come here to celebrate with the one person who had lit her world in a short space of time and she'd been daft to do it, to harbour a secret fantasy that dating him could become real.

That kiss had changed everything, had shifted the boundaries she'd been so desperate to establish and, no matter how hard she tried to act like it was nothing, it had been something. A cataclysmic something, a something every bit as incredible as what she'd imagined when their first kiss had been aborted all those years ago.

Taking one last look around the sensual, evocative room, she shook her head. She had to leave, get out of here while she still could, before he came home and she fell under his spell a little more.

Trying to convince her friends she was dating Bryce was one thing, falling into a trap of her own making another.

Snatching a notebook out of her handbag, she scrawled a quick note and stuck it on the glass-topped hall table. She needed time to marshal her defences, to cool things down between them.

As she slipped from the apartment, she had a feeling she'd need the entire Melbourne fire brigade to do that.

Bryce never bounded out of the lift. Unless he had some swank party to attend, that was. He hated coming home, preferring to stay out and about.

Old habits died hard.

His school days had been the same. Going home meant endless questions and probing and recriminations—or worse, if his dad was there on one of his rare shift changes from the hospital.

If the illustrious Victor Gibson happened to grace them with his presence there'd be the in-

evitable put-downs and condescension and disappointment.

How could the only child of a brilliant,
world-renowned obstetrician and a talented
midwife be so stupid? Easier to stay away and,
while he had no one nagging him these days,
he still preferred to spend as little time at home
as possible.

Not that the ultra-cool apartment Ballyhoo had
organised as part of his salary package felt like a
home. Every time he stepped through the thick,
shiny black door he felt as if he'd entered a film set.

Tonight was different. Tonight he had a spring
in his step and he whistled under his breath as
he opened the front door, for standing on the
other side of it was the most intriguing woman
he'd ever met.

'Eve, you here?'

Silence greeted him as he dumped his leather
satchel at the door and bumped it shut with his
hip, frowning as he glanced at his watch.

He'd come up the private lift from the underground car park so he hadn't checked with the

doorman if she'd arrived yet. Considering the late hour, she should've been here ages ago after he'd rung and said he'd be running late.

'Eve?'

Slipping out of his suit jacket, he swung it over his shoulder and, in doing so, knocked a piece of paper off the hall table. Picking it up, he scanned the cursive, flowing script, taking his time, as he always did.

Hi Bryce,
Sorry I couldn't wait around. Took a call, had to leave on business. You know how it is.
Speak soon.
Eve

He should've been relieved. Things were getting a little too cosy between them if he was the only person she wanted to celebrate with after landing a big event.

Combine that with the odd glances she'd been sneaking him when she thought he wasn't looking, and the way she'd responded to his impromptu kiss at the rehearsal dinner, and he should definitely be relieved.

Why the utterly deflating disappointment?

He couldn't get in too deep with Eve. When she discovered his secret—inevitable if they got together for real—he couldn't stand her pity. An intelligent, successful woman like her would definitely pity him, and if there was one thing he hated more than people judging him, it was their pity.

It was better this way.

While she'd cited business as an excuse to leave, he knew better. She'd sounded genuinely eager to see him on the phone earlier, her excitement audible. He understood. He got the same buzz when he nailed a pitch, wanted to shout it to the world.

Her invitation for a drink had surprised him, when he'd expected her to retreat after that kiss last night. The kiss he should've followed through on eight years ago, when he'd been a naïve jerk hell-bent on hiding his secret from those who knew him by doing what he did best: playing the fool.

He'd bet every dollar he had that, once the initial high had worn off, she'd arrived here and started second-guessing: him, the kiss, everything.

Not that he could blame her; he'd been doing a fair amount of that himself since last night. While he'd quashed his second thoughts at the wisdom of this dating game in deference to his all-important career, and achieving the goal that might change things between them, Eve obviously hadn't.

She'd bolted. He should be grateful; it gave him an uninterrupted evening to put in some solid work hours.

Crumpling the note in his hand, he lobbed it into the nearby bin and headed for the phone.

Takeout for one tonight; just the way he liked it.

Then why the bitter taste in his mouth?

CHAPTER EIGHT

'HAVING fun?'

With Bryce's breath fanning her ear, Eve stiffened before forcing herself to relax as she turned towards him.

'Sure. The ceremony went off without a hitch, I didn't trip up the aisle and take out the rest of the bridesmaids and this reception is amazing, so you bet I'm having fun.'

'This tells me otherwise.'

He reached out and smoothed a finger across her brow, gently, slowly, the simplest of touches, setting her skin alight. 'You were frowning.'

Damn, she'd thought she'd mastered her cool, unflappable face. Looked as if it was about as successful as her efforts to shield her heart against this incredibly sexy man dressed in a designer tux staring at her with concern.

Relieved when he stopped touching her, she shrugged. 'It's the events coordinator in me. Guess I keep wondering how the staff here managed to pull this off.'

By his dubious expression he didn't buy her excuse for a second but let it slide. 'The Melbourne Aquarium is an interesting location for a wedding reception.'

'I've done other functions here, corporate cocktails and team-building sessions, but never a wedding. It has a certain something, don't you think?'

'If you like being in an underground room sur-rounded by floor-to-ceiling water, separated from man-eating sharks and stingrays and a host of un-appealing deep-sea nasties by what appears to be the thinnest of glass, sure, it has an ambience.'

She laughed at his tortured expression. 'I forgot you don't like the ocean.'

'Who told you that?'

Puzzled by his wary tone, she shrugged. 'Tony

must've mentioned it. Or maybe the way you piked on our regular jaunts down to the coast gave it away.'

A clear image flashed across her mind of Bryce strutting in the back door of their family home, catching sight of their duffel bags loaded with crisps and sodas and sunscreen, boogie boards propped nearby, and taking a step backward.

He'd begged off that trip to the beach and every one after, and she'd put it down to her unwelcome presence as the one and only time he'd gone down to the Peninsula had been with Tony.

Aiming to lighten the mood, she punched him lightly in the arm. 'Not that I blame you. Let me guess, Tony made you navigator like he did me. I hated reading all those maps and signs with him demanding constant updates on our location.'

Rather than smiling as she expected, his lips thinned. 'Yeah, me too.'

The band started up their first set at that moment and, before she could make a quick escape—dancing up close and personal with Bryce would be pure torture, considering her decision to cool it after that kiss—he slipped his hand into hers.

'Come on, let's dance.'

She couldn't say no. Not with him tugging on her hand as he strode to the makeshift dance floor set in one of the tunnels with water all around, not with the blood pounding through her veins and drowning out every common sense reason why she shouldn't, and certainly not with her feet flying to keep up with the inner happy dance she was already doing.

Slipping one arm around her waist and holding her other hand with the lightest of pressure, he tugged her closer until their bodies brushed, her breasts skimming his chest, their thighs touching, the current buzzing between them having little to do with the static electricity of their clothes and everything to do with the underlying physical attraction between them that wouldn't quit, no matter how much she tried to ignore it.

'Now, this is more like it,' he murmured, moving his feet in time to the music, guiding her with an expertise she'd expect from a guy used to socialising.

The guys she knew, including AJ, Duane and Anton, who stood off to one side nursing beers, would rather bungee jump naked from the top of the Rialto building than dance so Bryce's sudden urge to trip the light fantastic had been a decisive escape from their conversation.

She'd clearly made him uncomfortable, discussing the past. Not that she could blame him. It wasn't a time she particularly enjoyed revisiting. But there'd been something more behind his reticence, something that might explain why he'd done such an abrupt turnaround from treating her with respect years earlier to going cold in front of his friends to showering her with warm affection now.

It wasn't an act, no matter how hard she'd tried convincing herself otherwise. You couldn't fake that kind of thing and his gregarious, spontaneous personality oozed genuine warmth, most of it directed at her. What chance did a girl have of shielding her heart?

'Relax, you're tensing up.'

His hand slid from her waist up her back, stroking her, burning a trail through the flimsy chiffon of her bridesmaid dress.

He expected her to relax when he was doing *that?*

His fingertips skimmed her spine, sending delicious tingles spreading through her body like the far-reaching tentacles of the octopus swimming lazily by without a backward glance.

She bit down on her lip as he dipped his head, his warm breath tickling her ear, his masculine scent combined with the faintest citrus filling her senses until she swayed, punch-drunk on sensation, in tune with him far more than the music.

'There are some definite perks to being your date.' His hand released hers to trail down her bare arm before linking with the other behind her back, circling her, holding her, cherishing her while she secretly wished he'd never let go.

'Dancing being one of them?'

Brushing the barest of butterfly kisses against

her temple, he said, 'Holding you like this being one of them.'

She managed a mute nod, unable to speak as a sudden lump of emotion lodged in her throat.

When he held her like this, touched her like this, spoke to her like this, she felt special, desirable and for that one infinitesimal moment she forgot all the reasons why she shouldn't be in his arms and gave herself over to the sheer unbridled pleasure of it.

'You dance like a dream.' His head dipped, his cheek grazed her temple, his body swayed in perfect sync with hers and she sighed, swept away in a fantasy they were dating for real.

Closing her eyes, she rested her head against his shoulder, savouring his proximity, the subtle citrus scent embedded in the fine wool of his tux, his soft hum in tune with the old dance hit reverberating through his chest.

The perfect moment, with the perfect man…

She, of all people, knew there was no such thing as perfect.

Her eyes fluttered open as she reluctantly lifted

her head, wishing she could capture this frag-
ment in time for ever, a treasured memory to re-
surrect on one of those long winter evenings
when she liked to curl up on the couch in front
of the open fire sipping her favourite cocoa.

She loved those evenings: the peace, the
cosiness, the freedom to relax in her oldest yoga
pants and T-shirt, make-up-less, with her glasses
sliding down her nose like they always had.

But she'd be lying if she didn't wish for
someone to share it all with and being held in the
protective circle of Bryce's strong arms, with his
male scent infusing her senses and the welcome
warmth radiating off his body bamboozling her,
resurrected that wish in an instant.

'Don't you hate it when the song has to end?'

He smoothed her hair back, his fingertips en-
twining through the strands, gently massaging
her scalp and she shivered involuntarily, his
touch eliciting a fiery need in the deepest
recesses of her neglected body.

With what was probably a practised touch, with
those incredible blue eyes wide with desire and

a small sexy smile playing about his lips, she knew, whatever she may wish for in the heat of the moment, Bryce wasn't it.

He couldn't be, no matter how much she wanted him for real.

She slipped out of his arms. 'Everything has to end some time.'

He scanned her face, a tiny crease appearing between his brows, and she quickly mustered a smile.

'Come on. I think dessert's being served.' She turned on her heel and headed towards their table, silently cursing her foolishness in falling for a guy who would run a mile if he saw deep down she hadn't changed a bit, still harboured a giant crush that, if anything, had increased with age.

Bryce pulled up outside Eve's house and switched off the engine. He wanted her to invite him in. He willed her to do it, hoping she wanted to explore this connection they shared as much as he did.

As she turned towards him, her expression closed, her eyes guarded, he knew the only place he was headed tonight was his cold, empty apartment.

'Thanks for tonight. I had a great time.'

Trite words, general words she could've said many times to countless other guys. Empty words with a distinct hollow ring, when what he wanted to hear spill from her lush mouth were genuine words of warmth and excitement and honesty in recognition of this undeniable attraction simmering between them, despite their initial platonic deal.

He could've answered in the same *I did too* vein but he hadn't got this far in life without taking risks and he'd be damned if he sat here and pretended there was nothing between them.

'I'm not going to play this game, Eve.'

Her pupils dilated, large and dark, wide with alarm, as her glossed lips parted in a small surprised O.

'What game?'

'The one where we dance around each other, hiding behind this dating deal we made, when we both know damn well there's more going on.'

There, he'd said it, put it out there, demanding a reaction, a recognition she felt half as bemused by all this as he did.

She quickly averted her gaze, staring out the windscreen at the deserted street, her fingers fidgeting with the hem on the slinky dress that had driven him wild all day. Or, more precisely, the way her lithe body had filled it out so perfectly.

The few weddings he'd been to, the bridesmaids had worn boring satin numbers in Godawful bright colours, but the soft pale-pink dress draping Eve's body had shifted and shimmered as she moved, making him itch to touch it, see if it felt as soft as it looked, to touch her.

'There's nothing going on.'

'Liar,' he murmured, leaning across to capture her chin, his touch insisting she look at him.

Words were cheap but her eyes couldn't lie. Not those wide, dark brown pools of honesty. She used to hide them behind glasses but not any more and he'd seen how much she wanted him: after their first dinner, their first kiss, and tonight, their first dance.

He waited, unaware he was holding his breath as her gaze fixed on his bow tie, moved upwards with slow regret until their gazes collided, his blunt and assessing, hers shadowed and reluctant. But the shutters didn't last and the second the dark chocolate melted into warm desire he breached the short distance between them and kissed her.

Their first kiss might've initially been a prove-a-point kiss that quickly got out of control but this one was wild from the start, a no-holds-barred, candid kiss from the heart, filled with passion and wonder and soul-deep need.

She made a soft mewling sound as he slanted his mouth across hers repeatedly, her hands clutching his lapels as she pulled him closer, opening her lips beneath his, meeting him halfway, pressing against him with urgency.

He'd wanted an honest answer—looked like he had it—as his tongue traced the soft fullness of her lips, sweeping into her mouth, exploring, teasing and she gave herself wholeheartedly in return, her mouth ravenous, demanding a response he was more than happy to give.

Blood pounded through him, coursing through his veins hard and fast, impossible to slow or steady. Not that he wanted to.

This was what he'd been fantasising about since the first time he'd tasted her sweet lips, this pulsing, passionate, very real expression of how she was feeling, a frank response that she wanted him as much as he wanted her.

She trembled, her breath coming in short, soft pants as he slid his mouth across her cheek, feathering tiny kisses all the way to her ear before ducking down her neck in slow, exquisite detail.

His body ached for her, his pulse quickening as she released his lapels to slide upwards, her fingertips skimming his face, exploring it with delicate finesse before trailing downwards again, toying with his collar, tugging on his tie.

'Eve?'

'Hmm?'

Her lips found the pulse point in his neck and he groaned, letting his head fall back as her tongue traced tiny circles, her mouth nipping him until he thought he'd combust on the spot.

'You know this isn't faking it, right?'

She stilled on a reluctant sigh, her mouth ceasing its playful exploration, and he instantly wished he hadn't spoken.

But he had to know, had to make sure she wasn't doing this out of some warped sense of cementing their deal, had to ensure it was all about him and how he made her feel rather than guaranteeing he stuck around to convince her friends they were a couple.

'Define faking it.'

Her forced chuckle sounded exactly that, forced, and he cradled her face in his hands, leaving her no option but to meet his gaze head-on.

'I don't know about you, but somewhere along the line this dating scheme of yours has gone beyond platonic. Guess I was wondering how you feel about that.'

Her eyes searched his—for what? Reassurance? Sincerity?

Hell, he'd had no intention of getting involved

with her at the start. He never got involved with anyone, preferring to keep his love life tangle-free. A huge misnomer—*his love life.*

He didn't do love. Too complicated, too messy and too revealing, for there was nothing surer than his secret getting out if he let a woman get too close.

She'd almost slipped under his guard the night of Tony's party but he'd prevented it by acting so awfully.

So what was he doing cosying up to her now? She was smart, wouldn't take long before she guessed why he'd fled all those years ago, why he had every intention of keeping her at arm's length now.

But he couldn't stop this…this…*thing* between them. Ignoring their attraction would be like admitting failure on a campaign and the chances of that happening were a big fat nil. He'd started down this road of honesty. He'd have to take it all the way.

Her eyes shimmered with wariness but she had nowhere else to look and, as she met his gaze, he saw exactly what he'd been hoping for: blatant desire.

She wanted him as much as he wanted her, but would she admit it?

'I don't want this to get too intense,' she said softly, her lower lip trembling, undoing his resolve to push her.

'It doesn't have to be.'

He dropped his hands, shook his head at potentially making a mess of this.

'I just wanted you to know I'm not jerking you around.'

He ran a hand through his hair, wishing he was more articulate. How was it he could nail a pitch with his eyes closed, yet couldn't string two coherent words together in front of this savvy woman?

'What I mean is I'm not taking advantage of our deal and playing up to you just for the hell of it. I like being with you. For real.'

She didn't say a word. Instead, she reached out and slid her fingers through his, squeezing his hand gently.

'Thanks for being honest. I'm enjoying this too. But I don't want it to get complicated.'

His jubilation at her admission evaporated in an instant. 'What's complicated?'

She didn't like confrontation. He could see it in her look-away glance, her fiddling fingers as they plucked at the hem of her dress, the rigidity of her slim shoulders.

'I don't have time for a relationship. It's not what I want right now so, yes, I acknowledge we've got a spark but I think we leave it at that.'

A spark? Very understated considering they'd almost ripped each other's clothes off a few moments earlier.

He should leave it alone but he couldn't, spurred on by an uncharacteristic urge to push her for answers he could barely contemplate himself.

'So we keep going as we have been? Dating for the next month and that's it?'

She hesitated and, in that split second before she dropped her gaze to stare at her white-knuckled clenched hands, he glimpsed pure unadulterated fear.

What had her running scared? So scared she wasn't willing to take a chance on having a little fun?

'That's it.'

Her soft, tremulous words echoed in the car, a cloak of vulnerability shrouding her shoulders like the finest mink.

He wanted to bundle her into his arms and comfort her but, considering how much he wanted her, touching her right now wouldn't be the brightest thing he'd ever done so he settled for hiding his true feelings as he always did: with quick wit.

'In that case, let me escort my date to the front door before this car turns into a pumpkin and I trade the tux for a frog suit.'

She smiled as something indefinable and infinitely scary shifted in the vicinity of his heart.

She was right.

They had to stick to the original plan.

Contemplating anything else would be crazy.

CHAPTER NINE

EVE braced herself for the oncoming onslaught as she spied the bridal babes weaving their way through the picnic tables, gazes determined, smiles resolute.

Not that she blamed them. She'd done a fine job of avoiding them so far, staying glued to Bryce's side, hanging on his every word, feigning interest in the corny decorations featuring intertwining As and Ms festooning the place.

Ironic, considering Bryce was the last person she wanted to be close to after last night.

That kiss in his car after the wedding had been an unmitigated disaster. Not the kiss itself. That had been spectacular. It was the aftermath that had her cringing and wishing she'd never devised this zany scheme in the first place.

If their first kiss at the rehearsal dinner had shocked her, their second had sent her good intentions to hold him at arm's length up in a sizzle of lust.

She'd gone from independent career woman secure in her home and business to yearning romantic mess who craved a guy totally wrong for her with a passion. A strong, unquenchable passion that throbbed and blossomed and grew as she stood here, watching him chat with the guys like they'd been mates for ever.

She'd tried so hard to keep her burgeoning crush under control, fooling herself into believing that first kiss at the rehearsal dinner had been all show, an attempt on both their parts to authenticate their dating.

It had worked until that mind-blowing kiss in the car last night. They hadn't been on show then, so every astonishing, scintillating second had been all about them—pure pleasurable delight. She tingled all over from the memory alone and, struggle as she might, she couldn't wipe the grin off her face as the girls approached.

'Well, well, will you look at that? Someone's looking mighty pleased with herself.'

Mattie sidled up to her and handed her a glass of champagne. 'Not that I blame you, hon. The more I see of Bryce, the more I understand why you haven't dated much.'

Carol popped an olive in her mouth, swirling the rest of her Martini. 'Yeah, you've been waiting for top notch rather than wasting time dating dregs.'

Eve laughed. 'You girls haven't done too badly yourselves.'

She gestured towards the barbecue where AJ, Duane, Anton and Bryce were raising beer bottles in a toast of some sort.

Carol sighed, a dreamy look on her face. 'Looks like we've all hit the jackpot.'

Guilt pierced Eve, niggling like a deep spur, but now wasn't the time or place to tell the girls the truth. Mattie was still floating, the guys were bonding and she couldn't take the risk of them thinking badly of Bryce.

She'd got them into this; he'd been good enough to help her out. What would her friends think when they learned the truth? Worse, what if the guys felt that they'd been duped and ostracised him from the business community completely?

An awful thought insinuated its way into her brain—something she hadn't considered when she'd first hatched this scheme. Bryce needed to make contacts in Melbourne and she'd dangled AJ, Anton and Duane in front of him for that purpose. But what if it all went horribly wrong when she told the girls the truth and the guys tarnished his business reputation? All three had the power to make Bryce's name mud in Melbourne; where would he be then?

Heck, she couldn't tell the girls, not now, no matter how much it grated to hide the truth from them.

Then again, what was the truth?

Watching Bryce throw back his head and let out a belly laugh, she couldn't ignore the insistent feeling she was dating him for real, despite all protests to the contrary.

'Hey, what's up?'

Mattie placed a hand on her arm as Eve wrenched her gaze away from Bryce, needing some sound relationship advice for the first time in her life.

'Can I ask you girls something?'

'Anything,' they said in unison, chuckling as they linked pinkies in a jinx sign girls the world over did at primary school.

Eve knew she was taking a risk. In asking the girls her question, she was risking revealing a part of her deepest insecurities. And that was scary. Beyond scary.

The bridal babes had never seen her anything other than confident, cool, successful, a city girl on top of her game. They did brunches, met up for snatched lattes over BlackBerrys, had cocktails to catch up on gossip. She'd cooked gourmet dinners for them, went to the ballet, shared a laugh at salsa lessons.

But she'd never revealed her old insecurities to her friends, never told them how she'd deliberately chosen a career that thrust her into a social whirlwind because being surrounded by beautiful things, beautiful people, made her feel beautiful.

She'd never told them that a few hours of intense male attention at a party eight years ago had transformed her life, had made her yearn to feel that good all the time, had propelled her into making life choices that she revelled in every day, yet she was still the same shy girl deep down, petrified Bryce would walk again if he discovered the real her.

'Wow, this looks serious.'

Linda slung an arm over her shoulder while beckoning Mattie and Carol closer. 'This could be something really important, like a birds and bees question.'

They all cracked up and Eve sent her intuitive friend a grateful look for breaking the tension.

'Actually, you'll probably laugh at this, but I was wondering when you girls let your partners see the real you.'

'The real me?' Mattie wrinkled her nose as if the thought of AJ seeing her in anything other than her favoured Gucci was totally foreign.

'You know,' Eve persisted, 'without make-up, in around the house clothes, with your hair unstyled and not looking the glamorous goddesses you usually are.'

Carol frowned and patted her sleek bob. 'Oh, you mean *that* real!'

Silence descended on the group as they pondered the question, while Eve shifted her weight from heel to heel. Was it so difficult to answer?

'Well?'

'I'm thinking.'

Linda tapped her red lipsticked mouth with a matching fingernail. 'I think I dropped the whole make-up thing at home with Anton within the first month.'

Fear lanced Eve, swift and sharp. She could never contemplate showing any guy, let alone Bryce, the real her in that amount of time. Ironic, considering that was the amount of time she had with him if they stuck firmly to their deal.

Mattie's perfectly plucked eyebrows shot heavenwards. 'That soon? Heck, I don't think AJ saw me without make-up till we were engaged.'

'Really?'

Carol held her French-manicured nails at length, studying them intently. 'Well, I don't think Duane's ever seen me totally au naturale.'

'What?'

Once again, they spoke in unison, though this time there were no jinx signs. They were too focused on their perfectly polished friend without a hair out of place.

Carol shrugged. 'I believe in always being well-groomed for your husband. Keeps them interested, you know.'

Mattie shook her head. 'Girlfriend, you sound like you've just stepped off the Ark! And, in case you haven't noticed, Duane thinks you walk on water, so he'd love you whether you wore make-up or turned green like the Incredible Hulk.'

'Nothing wrong with being well presented.' Carol must've noticed her expression. 'Right, Eve?'

She couldn't agree more. People looked at you differently when you were well presented, they treated you differently, they thought you were a somebody rather than a nobody, no matter how smart you were.

She knew that better than anybody and, while Carol's response didn't reassure her, what Linda and Mattie had said struck a chord.

'If you're worried about Bryce, don't be. Anyone can see he adores you.'

The tiny bud of hope deep within her heart unfurled its petals a smidgeon. Was he that good an actor? Was he merely playing the dating role she'd assigned him or did he feel something for her? His actions and words last night implied he did, especially as they hadn't been on display for her friends.

'Yeah, he gets the look whenever you're with him,' Linda said, nodding.

'What look?'

Mattie patted her cheek. 'The "I'm smitten and don't know what the hell to do about it" look. We've all seen it before.'

Yeah, on your guys, not mine, she thought, managing a breezy smile as the man in question chose that moment to catch her gaze across the garden and sent her a cheeky wink.

'See? Smitten,' Mattie said smugly. 'Relax, hon, it may be early days for you two but he's a keeper. I have a feeling the babelicious Bryce won't blink an eye if you strut around with mud on your face and a garbage bag for a dress.'

And, just like that, some of Eve's old insecurities receded. What if she was making too much of this, letting old insecurities stand in the way of her happiness? Right now, Bryce made her happy. And she had a feeling that if she let go of her reservations, she could be the happiest she'd ever been.

'Thanks,' she said, downing the rest of her champagne, buoyed by her new determination.

She was going to do it.

Tell Bryce she wanted to date him—for real.

Chuckling, the babes linked arms along with her. 'Come on, let's grab a champagne top-up before we wander over to that barbecue where there are some seriously hot guys with our names stamped all over them.'

I wish, Eve thought as she happily wandered towards the bar with her friends, *I wish.*

Bryce watched Charlie's Angels flutter around Eve like busy butterflies, each exotic and beautiful in their own way.

As attractive as they might be, they couldn't compete with the gorgeous woman in their midst, looking cool and elegant and oh-so-delectable. He wanted her with a staggering fierceness and, while she didn't want anything beyond their dating deal, he had other ideas.

It wasn't as if he was proposing marriage. They could date for the month she'd stipulated and walk away at the end. He never dated longer than that usually anyway, so this thing with Eve wouldn't be any different.

A win-win for them both.

Then why did he feel like a loser at the thought of walking away from her again?

'So, Bryce, I hear you're working for Ballyhoo these days?'

Nodding, he focused his attention on AJ. 'Yeah, it's a great opportunity.'

AJ nursed a beer and ran a hand across his chin. 'I may have another one for you. Hot Pursuit's advertising contract is up for grabs. I've never used Ballyhoo before but you seem like a stand up guy. How'd you like a shot at it?'

A shot at one of the biggest ad contracts in Australia? He refrained from punching the air and letting out a whoop—just.

'That'd be great. Thanks, mate.'

Much more sedate, much more professional but AJ must've sensed his jubilation for he grinned and raised his beer bottle in his direction.

'No worries. Ring my PA and tee up an appointment. Just so you know, we've got three other companies vying for it and the pitches are scheduled for next month. Timeline not too short?'

Not at all, not if he worked night and day between now and then. And he would, for this was the break he was looking for.

When he'd agreed to Eve's outlandish scheme, he'd hoped to make contacts but never in his wildest dreams had he expected to be given an opportunity like this.

If he could land the Hot Pursuit contract his career would shoot into the stratosphere. Landing the ad campaign for Australia's biggest sporting company could only lead to international work. He'd be set for life, would reach his goal, with his past well and truly behind him.

Clinking his beer bottle against AJ's, he said, 'I like working to tight deadlines. It won't be a problem.'

'Good. I'm looking forward to seeing what you come up with.'

Chugging back his beer, AJ's gaze wandered to the women.

'And don't think this has anything to do with Eve. She didn't ask me for any favours and, even if she did, I don't let my personal life mix with business. I've checked into you, like what I've heard and as we've hung out a few times…' he shrugged '…I'm interested in seeing your work. Now, if you don't mind, I see my new bride making eyes at me. Later.'

As Bryce watched AJ make a beeline for Mattie, his jubilation evaporated. He'd been so busy doing mental high-fives he'd completely forgotten about Eve and what this could mean for them.

Once he reached his goal, he would have no excuses not to pursue her.

His goal had been the reason he'd steered clear of commitment, hadn't been interested in anything other than dating all this time, but now, achieving the ultimate success in business had the potential to lead to his ultimate downfall.

Hell, he hadn't thought this through.

Wanting to pursue her, to see if the attraction between them could explode into a raging inferno of passion for the month they were together was one thing. Achieving his dream and discovering a woman who could make the rest of his secret dreams come true was another.

His brain whirred with the ramifications of nailing this pitch and while a small part of him said leave it, the driven, proud part of him that had struggled for recognition his entire life screamed that he had a brilliant opportunity, one he couldn't afford to pass up.

As he watched Eve flick her shiny brown hair over her shoulder and laugh at something AJ said, he knew what he had to do.

Concentrate on business. Cool things off with Eve, despite the insane urge to do otherwise. And if he nailed the pitch, reached his goal, he'd worry about the rest of his dreams then.

Eve willed the miles between AJ's bayside mansion and her place away.

She had a plan. Get home, whip up her favourite prosciutto-wrapped chicken breast with fennel butter, followed by sticky date pudding and then subtly—or not—tell Bryce she'd changed her mind.

She wanted to date him, every scrumptious inch.

His many facets intrigued her—suave and confident one minute, fun-loving and boyish the next. He'd slotted into the gang as if he'd known them for years, and while she'd wanted a date to impress them, he'd far surpassed expectations.

'You're awfully quiet.' He indicated, checked over his shoulder in his blind spot and pulled off the freeway. 'In fact, you've been silent the whole trip.'

'Just thinking.' If he only knew. 'I could say the same about you.'

'Business on the brain. You know how it is.'

'Yeah, I do.'

Though, lately, Soirée hadn't been occupying all her thoughts as it usually did. Uh-uh, he had pride of place there, easily superseding the upcoming AFL gala and the Spring Racing Carnival bonanza she had planned.

Her house came into view as he drove up the street, the cream-rendered bricks, Brunswick-green trim and terracotta window frames giving her a warm thrill, the same secure, satisfied feeling she had every day when she arrived home after a hard day's work.

'Would you like to—'

'I have to—'

They laughed and he waved his hand towards her. 'Ladies first.'

'I was wondering if you'd like to come in. I can whip up some dinner. Open a bottle of wine. Unwind a bit.'

His smile faded, his expression guarded, the first time he'd looked at her with anything other than warmth. 'Thanks, but I can't. I've got loads of work to do.'

'Right.'

She forced a smile while silently chastising herself for making such a hash of things last night. She'd told him she wasn't interested and he'd obviously taken her at her word.

'Another time, maybe?'

He paused, as if searching for the right words, and her heart sank further.

'AJ has given me a shot at pitching for Hot Pursuit's new ad campaign.'

She let out a long, low whistle through pursed lips. 'Wow, that's great. Congratulations.'

'I haven't done anything yet. Which is why I need to get my butt into gear. I have less than a month to come up with the winning pitch.'

'Bet you'll do a brilliant job.'

She had no doubts. She'd Googled him when she'd first seen that Net article, had read up on his stellar career and lightning-fast rise to the top of the ad world. He'd taken Sydney by storm, bursting onto the scene from nowhere and now he had his sights set on Melbourne.

She should be thankful. He'd never have agreed to pose as her date if she hadn't dangled the contacts in front of him. She should be downright ecstatic her introductions had gone so well. Instead, she had the faintest sour feeling that now he had what he wanted he couldn't wait to see the back of her.

'We're still on for the launch party next week?'

His slow nod added to her growing foreboding. 'I'll have to see how things go work-wise. If I've got the basics down for the pitch, we'll go. Otherwise, I'll have to give it a miss.'

'That's fine.'

It wasn't and her impending sense of doom increased when he glanced at his watch, as if she was taking up too much of his precious time.

Slinging her bag over her shoulder, she opened the door. 'Thanks for accompanying me today.'

'My pleasure.'

Hating how needy she sounded, she said, 'I'll

call you and let you know when the cocktail party for the video night is scheduled. Mattie isn't sure if they'll take a few extra days on their honeymoon or come back early for AJ's launch so she said she'd confirm by e-mail. Is that okay?'

'Sure.'

Sadness seeped into her heart, warring with embarrassment, making it ache the same way it had that night he'd turned his back and walked away from her.

Actually, no, this was worse—much worse. Back then, she hadn't known how wonderful he was, how warm and spontaneous and funny. Now she knew, having him shut down on her, using monosyllables for responses rather than the ribbing she'd grown accustomed to, hurt. More than it should.

'Bye.'

She held up a hand and almost tumbled out of the car in her haste to leave.

'Eve?'

Biting down on her bottom lip to stop it quivering, she forced herself to turn around.

'Yeah?'

'Thanks.'

Dusk cast long shadows over his car, over his face and she couldn't see his expression in the growing darkness so she had no idea if the wistful regret in his voice was real or a figment of her wishful imagination. 'For what?'

'For understanding.'

Nodding, she spun on her heel and headed for the door.

Understanding?

She didn't understand any of this, least of all the devastation wreaking havoc on her emotions as he gunned the engine and slid away from the kerb.

CHAPTER TEN

BRYCE shut down his PowerPoint presentation, scanning the conference table for some sign that his initial pitch wasn't complete rubbish.

Sol's ruddy face remained impassive, while Davin's complexion turned a pale shade of green, clear indication his presentation couldn't have been all bad.

'That's my initial idea. Angus Kilbride has never used Ballyhoo before so I thought I'd go in bold, with a fresh, new, in-your-face campaign. What do you think?'

Pin-drop silence, punctuated by the quiet shuffling of papers. No one wanted to say a thing, waiting for Sol to pronounce judgement before they backed him up like lapdogs.

He'd seen it all before. Creative copywriters waiting for the go-ahead before letting their imaginations run free, execs holding their breath for approval.

He'd been there, done that but this meant a whole lot more. Sol's endorsement of his Hot Pursuit pitch would make or break his career in Melbourne. The big guy had spelled it out for him and he'd make damn sure he delivered. Despite the potential minefield success would mean for his personal life.

Steepling his podgy fingers together, Sol leaned forward and fixed him with a probing stare.

'How soon can you get the rest done?'

'I'm working on it day and night.'

It consumed him, this quest to nail the Hot Pursuit contract. He'd always been driven, ever since he'd slaved nights to gain his high school diploma and, later, his economics degree.

No one had thought he could do it. He'd shown them all. And, when he secured this campaign, his professional reputation would be set. As for the rest…he'd decide what to do about the Eve situation when he reached his goal, not before.

Sol drummed his fingers together, his bulbous nose almost getting trapped between them, before he sat back and thumped his palms on the conference table with a decisive bang.

'Good work. And if you land this account it'll be nothing short of brilliant. Now, I want all of you to give Gibson whatever assistance he needs over the next fortnight to make this happen. Got that?'

Casting a look that meant business around the table, Sol left the room and everyone gave an audible sigh of relief.

Glowing inwardly from the high praise from a man of few words, he gathered up his laptop and presentation notes, eager to get cracking on the next stage of his pitch.

'Impressive.'

He glanced up at Davin, perched on the edge of the table, a sour-cum-smarmy expression on his face.

'Thanks.'

'How did you get an opportunity with Angus Kilbride? Rumour has it he's a hard nut to crack.'

'The usual meet and greet stuff. You know how it is.'

Davin's forehead crinkled in fake concentration. 'Actually, I don't. I've been scouting a meeting with the big guy for ages and no-go. Yet here you are, new to the Melbourne scene, and not only do you get to meet him, you get to pitch. Wish I knew your secret.'

'Hard work,' he bit out—*something you'd know nothing about.* 'Speaking of which, I have to get back to it. Later.'

Turning his back on Davin's speculative stare, he stalked from the conference room.

Thanks to Eve, he had a shot at this—a real shot. And how had he thanked her? By burying his nose in work—work he still needed to complete to nail this campaign. He'd missed her—really missed her—and it had only been a few days.

While he may have wowed the boss with his preliminary outline, he needed to take this all the way and that meant keeping his distance from a guaranteed distraction in the form of one luscious woman.

Then again, since when had he ever not taken a risk?

'Thought you were too busy to attend this launch party?'

Bryce handed Eve a champagne flute filled to the brim. 'It's work. Gives me a feel for the current mob Hot Pursuit are using, hopefully gives me an edge for my pitch.'

'Right. Work.'

She sipped at her champagne, her melted chocolate eyes fixed on him as if she could see right through him.

Work was the excuse he'd cited for being here while the beautiful woman with a knowing glint in her eyes and coy smile curving her lips saw it for the feeble lie it was.

He was here because of her, because he couldn't stay away, no matter how focused he was supposed to be on business, how terrified he was of achieving his goal and losing his excuse not to pursue her for real.

Biting back a grin the longer she stared at him with awareness making her eyes sparkle, he pointed to a giant billboard-size poster of the latest and greatest athletic shoe.

'See that? I'm feeling inspired just looking at it.'

Her smile widened as she lowered her champagne flute. 'Oh, really? And what type of slogan would you come up with for that? Have shoe—will travel?'

She tapped her bottom lip—her deliciously full, glossy bottom lip—as she pretended to think. 'These shoes were made for jogging and one of these days these shoes will run all over you?'

He chuckled as she snapped her fingers. 'I've got it. How about blue suede running shoes?'

'You've missed your calling. You should be in the ad business.'

She crooked her finger and he happily leaned forward, all too glad to inhale her soft vanilla fragrance, to have her arm brush against his jacket.

'And give you some stiff competition?'

Laughing, she patted his cheek. 'I wouldn't be that mean.'

Touching his cheek had been a joke, part of the word play, but the instant her soft palm scraped against him he wanted to haul her into his arms and have her touch him all over.

The thought inflamed him further and he needed a distraction, needed to deflect some of the heat back on to her. If not seeing her for a week did this to him, how the hell would he survive when their month came to an end?

When her hand dropped, he quickly grabbed it, sliding his fingers between hers and holding on tight.

'What's got into you?'

She blushed, glanced away. 'I don't know what you mean.'

Tipping up her chin so she had no option but to look at him, he said, 'I think you do.'

Her eyes widened with understanding before snapping shut, shutting out the heat flaring between them, the heat slowly simmering to burning point.

'You've been different tonight. More chatty, more lively, more at ease.' He squeezed her hand before drawing it up, unfurling her fingers from between his and placing a soft kiss on the palm. 'As for touching my cheek, you don't usually initiate physical contact, so I'll repeat the question. What's got into you?'

Curling her fingers over the kiss, he took pity on her, dazed expression and all, and released her hand. 'Not that I mind, but I'm curious. Does absence make the heart grow fonder?'

'You're teasing me.'

She rolled her eyes, but not before he'd glimpsed a shimmer of fear—genuine fear—as if he'd asked a question she had no hope of answering.

He'd known that feeling back in school way too many times to be comfortable. If she used a smart-assed comeback, he'd know she was floundering out of her depth as much as he used to.

'As for what's got into me, this stuff will do wonders for giving a girl false ideas of flirting grandeur.'

She raised her half-empty champagne glass in

a silent toast. 'With the absence thing, it's only been seven days, five hours and thirty-three minutes. Give a girl some time to miss you.'

Oh, yeah, she was definitely out of her depth. And if she kept looking at him with stars in her eyes, he'd know the feeling.

'There you go again. Cracking a funny.' Bending down, he whispered in her ear, 'Almost flirting!'

Batting her eyelashes, she pulled back enough to give him an outrageously false innocent look. 'Is it working?'

'Hell, yeah.'

Before he could think or rationalise or second-guess himself, he backed her into a nearby corner and kissed her, pouring all his pent-up frustration and desire and driving need into it.

God, he'd missed her. Missed being near her, missed hearing her laugh, missed basking in her warmth cloaked in the elegant cool only she did so well.

A small moan escaped her lips as he man-oeuvred them deeper into the shadows and he eased off the pressure, giving her a chance to stop this madness.

In response, her hands snaked around his neck, pulling his head closer, and he didn't need a second invitation as he took her mouth again, teased her lips apart, tasted her, feasted. His mouth was ravenous, his entire body on fire as they kissed as if there were no tomorrow.

But there was a tomorrow, and a day after that, and another after that, each and every day filled with work he couldn't lose sight of, no matter how tempting the distraction.

Gently disengaging, he leaned his forehead against hers, murmured, 'Wow.'

Her soft, ragged breathing did little to calm his libido and he reluctantly straightened, needing distance, needing perspective, needing a cold shower. A month's worth to cool his desire for the woman staring at him with the same dazed passion reflecting in his stare.

'You keep making a habit of that.'

'Some habits are harder to break than others.'

Dragging a hand through his hair, beyond rattled

when it shook slightly, he settled for thrusting it into his pocket to stop himself from reaching for her. 'And you, Eve Pemberton, are fast becoming one habit I'd very much like to keep.'

Her gobsmacked expression had him mentally slapping a hand over his mouth. Damn his hormones for making him run off at the mouth.

He should've kept this light-hearted, in the spirit of the casual flirting they'd been doing all evening. Instead, he'd blurted what he'd been thinking and now had to do some serious back-pedalling.

'Then again, I've learned to manage my habits, bad ones and all.'

Her hand crept up to her mouth, her fingertips absentmindedly touching her bottom lip, and he gritted his teeth to dampen the urge to do the same.

'Are you saying I'm bad for you?'

'I'm saying you're bad for my concentration.'

'And you need to concentrate right now because?'

'Work, remember? The reason I'm here.'

'The only reason?'

She wouldn't let him off the hook, damn it.

'Because, while this is coming up with perfectly logical rationale—' she pointed to his head '—this is having a hard time keeping up.'

She rubbed her thumb along his bottom lip and he bit back a groan, wondering where this temptress had emerged from, desperately needing the old Eve to put in an appearance right about now.

'No more kisses. Promise.'

'Too bad.'

With a last longing glance at his mouth, she sauntered away, leaving him cursing his impulse to come tonight, cursing her power over him and cursing the day he'd agreed to this stupid dating deal.

Eve knew he'd come after her.

Bryce was that sort of guy. Always up for a challenge. And she'd been stupid enough to issue one. All fine and dandy in the heat of the moment with his lips robbing her of all rational thought, but now her meagre supply of courage had run out, she was in trouble. Big trouble. The kind of trouble that couldn't be erased with more fake flirting or steamy eye contact.

She'd wanted to prove a point tonight, to show him she'd changed her mind about her *I don't want a relationship* stance.

What had she said to him in the car last week? Something along the lines of, 'I don't have time for a relationship. It's not what I want right now.'

Yeah, right. Not only had she changed her mind, she'd lost it completely. If the Silver Streak had worked a treat, the Red Peril she'd worn tonight was in a class of its own. Tight. Sprayed-on tight. Sleeveless, knee-skimming, cleavage-peeping. If the cut didn't grab a guy's attention, the colour would, the gorgeous pomegranate crimson making her stand out in a crowd of Melbourne black.

She'd never worn anything like it—probably wouldn't again—but, for tonight, for the last few hours, she'd felt like a different woman, had acted like a different woman.

If Bryce didn't get the idea now he never would and, when he came after her, she'd tell him. Once she'd downed another champagne or ten.

'Hey, wait up!'

He grabbed her arm, the instant sizzle of heat licking along her skin like an electric shock.

'I'm after a refill.' She held up her empty flute, knowing a bottomless glass wouldn't give her enough courage to carry through with the rest of her plan tonight. 'Back in a sec.'

'Eve, this isn't going to work.'

Her heart stalled, her confidence rapidly dwindling in the face of his sombreness.

'It's only another champagne—'

'You look amazing.' His gaze raked her body, set it alight, as she clutched her glass to stop herself from folding her arms over her chest where the evidence of just how much she burned for him was on clear show. '*You're* amazing but I can't do this right now.'

She could've pretended to misunderstand him again, could've made another joke but the time for kidding was over.

This was too important to her. *He* was too important to her.

'Why?'

His lips compressed, his determined stare bored into her, willing her to understand.

'Because nailing this pitch is critical.'

She clamped down on the little exasperated snort that escaped before she could stop it. 'Lots of people date and work. Most of the known universe, in fact.'

'Sorry, I have goals.' Shaking his head, he thrust his hands into his pockets. 'I can't afford the distraction.'

'Guess I should be flattered I can distract you.'

Her sarcasm elicited an instant response, mischief sparking his eyes.

'You could distract a monastery of meditating monks.'

Her mouth twitched at his analogy but she wouldn't let this go. She'd come this far; she would use up the last of her courage before she rehung the Red Peril in the closet and reverted to unruffled, non-confrontational Eve.

Jabbing a finger at him, she said, 'You're the one who's kissed me repeatedly and who's pulled back. What gives?'

'Kissing you was a mistake.'

'Oh, thanks very much,' she snapped, hating the blossoming hurt making her heart ache.

If she'd harboured any doubts she wasn't in over her head with this so-called platonic dating deal, the spreading pain in the vicinity of her masochistic heart put paid to that little delusion. Over her head? She was seriously drowning.

'I didn't mean it like that.'

He cupped her cheek, stroked it with his thumb and her heart lay down and waved a white flag in surrender.

'Kissing you was a mistake because I want to do it again and again and again. It's a mistake because I don't want to stop there.'

His hand dropped but his beseeching gaze never left hers. 'But, most of all, it's a mistake because when I kiss you I can't think of anything else and I can't afford that. Not now.'

Motivational music blared at that moment, loud and uncompromising, as AJ wandered onto a stage with several lithe models clad in minimal Lycra and Hot Pursuit's latest and greatest sneakers.

The fanfare didn't impress her but Bryce's eyes lit up as he scanned the scenario, taking it all in.

She had her answer right then.

'This is everything to you, isn't it? Winning this ad campaign?'

He tore his gaze from the stage, refocused on her and she knew his response before he spoke.

'I need to do this.'

'And us?'

Regret clouded his eyes. 'We carry on as we agreed at the start.'

Clamping down on the urge to rant and rave at the injustice of sticking to a stupid deal of her own invention, she nodded. 'Business as usual. Got it, loud and clear.'

This time when she walked away, she knew he wouldn't follow.

CHAPTER ELEVEN

EVE had cooked up a storm.

For the last four days straight.

When she wasn't at the office she was in the kitchen, taking out her frustrations by pummelling dough, tenderising meat and kneading pasta. All perfectly good venting activities involving loads of fist-thumping and hammering and wringing—the type of activities she'd like to practise on the man who'd caused this cooking frenzy in the first place.

The therapeutic cook-off hadn't worked. She was still mad—mad as hell. She was over it, over him.

Maybe not quite over him… Okay, okay, she had as much chance of getting over him as strolling down Chapel Street in her Ugg boots and tracksuit *sans* make-up.

Bryce blew hotter and colder than a Melbourne spring change. Kissing her one minute, citing business the next.

If he'd done it once she might've accepted his brush-off and believed he was a workaholic. But he'd done it several times, had hinted he wanted more from their dating deal at the rehearsal dinner with all that guff about plans evolving and changing, before backing off quicker than the boys she'd asked to take her to the prom.

It didn't add up.

She hadn't made it to the top of Melbourne's events consultancies without being able to read people and, right now, Bryce was hiding something.

For a moment she'd wondered if he was as fickle as she'd pegged him at Tony's party, ditching the nice act the moment he'd been given a shot at AJ's advertising contract, but common sense said otherwise.

By the heat of his kisses, his reluctance to stay away despite citing business, his reaction every time he kissed her, then backed off, she'd say he was torn.

Why? Darn it, none of this made sense.

She could always ask him.

Wrinkling her nose at the thought, she stirred the chilli con carne faster, moving the wooden spoon in concentric circles, the rhythmic action soothing, as always.

She did need to call him, to hand over some documents AJ had given her via Mattie. Her first reaction had been to fob them off but how would it look, a girlfriend not passing on documents to her boyfriend, who they assumed she'd see before them?

Prevaricating for the last few hours, she'd picked up the phone several times, only to drop the receiver and resume cooking, ignoring the pile of papers that taunted her from their place in the corner.

She had to hand over the documents, no choice; great, she'd known things would get complicated the longer she perpetuated this fraud.

With a defeatist groan, she propped the spoon

in its holder, turned down the stove and picked up the phone. Punching in the numbers, she waited, rearranging the spice rack with fiddling fingers as she gritted her teeth through the first ring…the second…the third…

'Hello?'

'Bryce, it's me.'

'Hey, Eve. How's it going?'

No hesitation, which had to be a good sign, right? And he sounded genuinely pleased to hear from her, another plus, so she ploughed on before she lost her cool.

'Great. Thought I'd give you a quick buzz and let you know AJ gave me some documents you might be interested in for your pitch.'

A pause followed—a long, loaded pause where her heart almost burst out of her chest. Even if he didn't want to see her, surely he'd want the documents for his all-important work?

'Thanks, I'll swing by and pick those up some time but right now I've got a ton of work to do.'

'Me too.'

'Look, I have to duck out and have dinner

anyway so why don't I drop by afterwards? Promise I won't stay long.'

Her gaze drifted to the simmering chilli on the stove, the tantalising aroma making her nose twitch. She'd cooked enough for a hungry posse; wouldn't it make sense to invite him to share as he'd be coming over anyway? How bad would it look when he dropped by, saw all the food and realised she hadn't asked him to dinner?

But sitting together at the table, sharing dinner, reeked of intimacy and he'd made it clear he wanted to keep his distance.

'Eve, if it's a problem, I can—'

'No problem. It's just that I've cooked a huge batch of chilli, so if you're busy with work, rather than wasting time ordering takeaway, why don't you eat here?'

He hesitated and she screwed up her face in embarrassment.

'Honestly? I've had my nose to the grindstone all day, I haven't had time to eat and the thought of your chilli is making me even hungrier.'

At least her cooking could achieve what she only dreamed about her body doing.

'In fact, I'm starving. I'll be there in half an hour. Do you want me to bring anything?'

You—only you.

Shaking herself out of her wishful reverie, she propped the phone between ear and shoulder as she opened the oven, donned mitts and slid freshly baked tortillas out.

'Yeah, a healthy appetite. I have enough food here for a small army.'

'A healthy appetite, huh?'

Her flushed cheeks had nothing to do with the wave of heat emanating from the oven and everything to do with the sudden shift in tone from light-hearted to sexy in a second.

Gulping, she desperately wished for a free hand to fan her scorching cheeks. 'Uh-huh. See you soon.'

She rang off and slid the baking tray onto the stove top before she burned her hands.

Considering the way she reacted to a simple

shift in Bryce's mood, she hoped that was the only thing at risk of being burned.

He was a sucker for a pretty face.

That was Bryce's excuse and he was sticking to it as he trudged up the manicured path to Eve's front door, hoping he didn't lose his cool completely and give in to this incessant, overwhelming need to make Eve his.

He'd been neck-deep in work when she'd called, cursing the phone when it broke his concentration, but the instant he'd heard her voice, warm and soft and tentative, he'd wanted to hang up and race to her house ASAP.

Sucker.

She stimulated on every level: intellectually, physically and, for the first time ever, emotionally.

He'd never had such a connection with anybody and it scared him. He'd always faced his fears—faced and conquered them—and he'd be damned if he let an inconsequential, irrational fear of falling for Eve stop him from being her friend.

It was the least he could do after she'd given

him this amazing opportunity through AJ and, while he may not be able to date her, why couldn't they hang out together as buddies?

Yeah, buddies. He could do that.

However, as she opened the front door to his knock, being buddies with this incredibly beautiful woman was the last thing on his mind.

'Hi, come on in.'

She held the door open and he struggled not to gape as the muted hall light streaked russet through her warm molasses hair, falling in disarray around her face. Her brown eyes shone with welcoming warmth and her designer jeans and T-shirt clung to her sleek frame as if they'd been poured on.

Breathtakingly, heart-stoppingly beautiful. Not in the classic sense of the word but, put together in a dazzling combination, Eve was all that and then some.

With a rueful smile, she rubbed her nose. 'Have I got a chilli smudge here?'

Mentally kicking himself for staring when he was supposed to be playing it cool, he shook his head. 'No, I think my eyes are glassy from staring at the computer screen too long. Sorry if I was rude.'

Her smile widened, genuine and perceptive; she didn't buy his woeful excuse and he didn't blame her. For someone good at thinking on his feet, that had been lame.

'Not at all. My eyes get that way too.'

Stepping into the hallway, the rich aroma of chilli and toasted bread filled the air and his tummy rumbled, reminding him of exactly how long it had been since he'd eaten.

'Sounds like someone's ready for dinner.'

She chuckled at his emphatic nod and ushered him through to the kitchen. 'We'll eat first, then I'll get you that paperwork.'

'Good idea,' he said, instantly entranced by the warmth, the smells and the vision of Eve totally at home behind the kitchen bench as he placed his load on a dresser in the corner.

He'd never had this. His mum's work hours at the hospital delivering babies had almost been as maniacal as his dad's and he'd rarely had a home-cooked meal. Not that he'd minded. The less he saw of his folks the better. The rare times they were home they'd only paid him cursory attention anyway, once they discovered he wasn't the child prodigy they'd hoped for.

Occasionally, after winning a pitch, in the quiet of his apartment, nursing a cold beer, he'd wonder if that was why he'd set himself the goal of achieving financial success before he would ever consider pursuing his secret dream—the warm, loving family he'd never had.

Did he equate success in his chosen field with being worthy enough to win the love of a good woman?

It had worked for his dad; his mum had eyes only for him, had barely acknowledged her only child and, while he'd shrugged off their unforgivable coldness growing up, he wondered if his yearning for a family the opposite of his was what drove him every day, what drove him towards his goal despite the deep-seated fear of what he'd have to risk once he achieved it.

'Need a hand?'

He headed for the island bench, propped himself on a stool and the warmth in her answering smile had him wanting to vault the bench and kiss her silly.

'Thanks, but I've got it covered. Fancy a wine?'

I fancy you.

His body clamoured to re-create the sparks they'd ignited with their kisses, to explore the heat simmering like their dinner on the stove. But he'd made his choice. Business over pleasure and he had to stick to it. Achieving his goal depended on it.

'I'd better not. Need to keep a clear head while I put the finishing touches on my presentation.'

She quirked an eyebrow as she ladled out chilli con carne into a serving dish. 'Wow, you have been working night and day if you're nearly finished.'

He gathered up the plates and cutlery, followed her to the cosy dining table, where he set two places before pulling out her chair.

'I'm manic when I have a deadline.'

'So I gathered. Tortilla?'

'Thanks.'

Somehow, his mention of work stifled their conversation and they ate in silence, the quiet punctuated with the odd 'pass the salt' or 'more water'.

As far as meals went, the food was fantastic but he missed the easy-going rapport they'd had when she'd cooked for him before, missed the sassy sparkle in her eyes, the playful smiles.

Then again, he wanted it this way, remember?

Buddies was good, anything more potentially disastrous.

This wasn't a good idea.

The fraught silence over dinner had bothered him so, rather than grabbing AJ's documents and making a run for it, he'd suggested he look over them here, over coffee.

One problem: how was a guy expected to concentrate on work when he had one big distraction wrapped up in a too-snug cardigan sitting opposite him?

It wasn't as if Eve was interrupting him, far from it. While he pretended to peruse the documents, Eve had sat down to work, ducking behind her laptop screen, tapping away on the keyboard, jotting down notes on a giant yellow notepad.

In fact, everything on her desk was yellow, from an oversized stapler to her Filofax, with a huge bunch of yellow roses in a clear cut-glass vase in the middle. It was a bright, sunny environment to work in, even on a darkening spring evening. He briefly wondered what she'd make of his work station at home: clear, functional, uncluttered.

He needed it that way to help him think, to help him use the methods he'd learned to optimise his performance. A performance in dire straits if he didn't concentrate on his presentation and not on the intriguing woman opposite.

He dropped his gaze back to the documents as she shifted in her seat but found his gaze unwittingly drifting upwards again when she resettled.

Picking up a pencil, she tapped it against her notepad, lost in thought, absentmindedly gnawing on her bottom lip, the action almost making him groan out loud with the frustration of how much he'd like to do the same.

Unfortunately, he must've made some sound because she looked up, her eyes wide and enquiring.

'Just thinking,' he said, linking his hands and stretching overhead, hoping she'd buy his nonchalant act.

Her gaze drifted to his chest and the spark of interest there had him wanting to drag her across the desk and into his arms, nonchalance be damned.

'How's it coming along?'

'Not bad.' He held up his Eee PC where he'd been making notes. 'This new software I'm using is great.'

'Anything I could use?'

Silently cursing his slip of the tongue, he shook his head. That was all he needed—for her to take a look at it and see why he used something like it.

'Doubt it, it's ad specific.'

'Okay.'

Her dubious glance had him gripping the end of the table to prevent himself from ducking around the other side and hugging her for sounding like a grouch.

'I don't know about you, but I've been at it all day and my brain's entering meltdown mode.'

She waved towards the screen, a slight frown puckering her brow. 'Me, too. The AFL are major league with their demands. Think I'm having a mini confidence crisis.'

'Don't. Your business success speaks for itself. You must be brilliant at what you do.'

Gratitude shimmered in her eyes before her gaze flickered back to the screen again. 'Thanks for the pep talk. I need it to pull this off.'

He studied her—so serious, so dedicated—and he was instantly transported back to their high school days when he'd wander into their kitchen with Tony, only to find Eve permanently seated at the table with her nose in a book. He'd always thought she was cute, even with those god-awful glasses and clothes she used to wear. Something about her eyes and her shy smile had tugged deep.

'What happened to your glasses?'

Her gaze snapped up to his, wary and shuttered. 'Contact lenses. More user-friendly.'

'I remember how you used to push those glasses up your nose constantly when they slid down.'

He also remembered how she'd bake choc-chip cookies for her dad, just because he liked them, how she'd buy sourdough bread because Tony wouldn't eat any other kind, how she'd managed to keep house and cook and excel at her studies, while having a ready smile and a kind word when Tony and her dad walked through the door.

She'd been amazing—was amazing—and he'd been a fool for hurting her the night of Tony's party, for letting her believe he didn't care, when he did.

'You remember?' Her eyebrows shot up at a rate of knots. 'That's right; you used to tease me about them.'

Remorse prickled him, along with a nasty urge to tell her the truth. But he couldn't. If he told her, she'd either pity him or go all soft and comforting. He was having a hard enough time holding her at bay now; what chance would he have if she turned soppy and wanted to hug him?

'I didn't call you four-eyes, though.'

'Bet you thought it.' She scrutinised him, her stare cool and assessing. 'Can I ask you something?'

'Sure.'

'Why did you acknowledge me at our place and not at school?'

Damn, he should never have gone down the reminiscing track. Now he'd have to make up something halfway plausible so that she wouldn't probe him for the truth.

'Because I was an obnoxious little jerk?'

She didn't buy his lame attempt at humour. 'Tell me why.'

Hell, she wouldn't let this go.

Pushing back from the desk, he placed the Eee PC on the desk and folded his arms. He'd have to opt for partial honesty. By the astute expression on her face, she wouldn't settle for anything less.

'Honestly? You intimidated me.'

'What?'

Her mouth dropped open, a surprised O.

'Crazy, huh? At home, you seemed more approachable. At school, you were this super-smart brain, always with your nose in a book and I was a goof-off, the kid who used his mouth to get a few laughs rather than get ahead. Guess I didn't want to run the risk of you cutting me down to size with some of those big words you knew.'

By the softening around her mouth and the appreciative gleam in her eyes, she believed him. Sad thing was, he almost wished he could tell her the rest—the real reason why she'd intimidated him.

That was what happened when you had a belly full of food and a woman staring at you with a scary mix of need and warmth and understanding in her entrancing chocolate-brown eyes.

'I would never have done that.'

She reached over and placed a comforting hand on his forearm and he gritted his teeth to stop himself from placing his hand over it.

'Yeah, but I was an egotistical brat. My behaviour had nothing to do with you. You asked why I did it; I told you. Now, do you mind if I get back to this?'

Their growing intimacy shattered with his

sharp comeback and she snatched her hand away before ducking behind her screen again.

'Fine.'

He'd hurt her. She'd only been concerned and he'd clammed up because she was getting too close.

He should be glad, for there'd been several tension-filled moments during dinner where he'd seen the need in her eyes, the passion bubbling below her cool exterior.

He'd almost given in, almost gone for it, despite the precious campaign. But his goal was ingrained, programmed into his psyche and he couldn't bomb, no matter how much he wanted her.

His jaw clenched, stifling the urge to explain, before he forced himself to relax. 'Eve, I'm sorry—'

'Don't be. I'm the one who's been a fool, hoping there was more to our friendship than my dating deal, trying to get a handle on what makes you tick, but hey, don't worry. I was obviously wrong.'

'This isn't what you think.'

Her gaze pierced him, fierce, angry.

'Then what is it?'

Shaking his head, he ran a hand through his hair, searching for the right words, his brain a scary jumble of letters and combinations he remembered all too well.

'Don't answer that. I know what's going on here. This dating thing is a business transaction, nothing more. I won't make the mistake of reading more into it again.'

He could've refuted it, could've blurted a truth he'd kept hidden from everyone for a lifetime but, instead, he nodded, shut down his small PC and picked up the paperwork.

She avoided looking at him as he stood and, while his feet urged him to make a run for it, he couldn't leave like this.

'Thanks for a great meal.'

He moved past her before stopping and laying a hand on her shoulder, his heart lurching when she stiffened. 'I wish things were different.'

He didn't stick around long enough to hear her whisper, 'Me, too'.

CHAPTER TWELVE

'YOU'VE got yourself a deal.'

Bryce stared at AJ, hoping his growing grin came across as professional and not goofy.

He'd done it.

His pitch had won Hot Pursuit's advertising campaign for the next year. All his hard work had paid off, all his sacrifices, namely losing any chance he had with Eve to benefit his career.

Was he happy? Hell, yeah, but the thought of what he'd potentially lost with Eve took the gloss off what should be a watershed moment.

'Great, thanks very much.'

He shook AJ's hand, sent a polite nod around the table at the sporting company's execs.

'We'll schedule another meeting for early next week to get the ball rolling, okay?'

Laughter followed AJ's statement as he tossed a football into the air and, once again, Bryce was struck by the mateship he'd seen in evidence at this company.

Sure, he hadn't been at Ballyhoo long but their meetings never had this kind of feel, a sincere camaraderie between colleagues who genuinely loved their job. Come to think of it, none of the agencies he'd worked at in Sydney had been like this either, but then the ad world was probably more cut-throat than sporting goods.

'I'll tee up the appointment.'

Gathering his presentation, he waved to the group. 'Nice meeting you all. Look forward to working with you.'

He left on a general chorus of goodbyes, waiting until he got outside the conference room to punch the air with a satisfying, 'Yes!'

He couldn't wait to get back to the office and tell Sol the good news.

His job was secure.

Until the next pitch.

The thought pulled him up short, garnering

strange looks from the young receptionist behind the front desk.

Where had that come from? He was used to the competitive nature of his field, usually thrived on it. What was different this time? He should be shouting his success from the top of his apartment building, yet something had taken the edge off his victory and he knew exactly what that was.

Eve.

He couldn't get her out of his head, particularly the hurt look in her eyes when they'd had dinner.

He'd avoided her since, citing work issues to soothe his niggling conscience. Not that she'd called and, considering the way they'd left things, she probably wouldn't. The cocktail party and wedding video night was tomorrow and after that she wouldn't want to see him again.

How easy it had sounded at the beginning: act as her date, walk away at the end with a few business contacts under his belt. He'd never expected to feel like this. Surprised, uncertain, scared, a stupid, irrational fear that in playing this dating game, he'd come out the loser.

He hadn't expected to like her this much, hadn't expected the kindling spark the night of Tony's party to still be there; worse, for it to flare to life in a scorching whoosh of flames that threatened to consume them both.

Sealing this deal had been a major goal. Not just establishing his reputation at Ballyhoo, but financially. Ever since he'd started work he'd had a plan. Reach five million in earnings and maybe he'd have something to offer a woman, enough for her to take a chance on him, encumbrances and all.

He'd plucked the figure out of the air at the time, not interested in a relationship with anyone, focused solely on success.

Now he'd achieved his goal. And there was a woman in the picture. A beautiful, intelligent woman he could now offer something to without guaranteed rejection. Not that money would matter to her—Eve was successful in her own right, had a lucrative business and a house in a posh suburb with all the trimmings—but it mattered to him in a non-mercenary, vindicating achievement way. He'd battled long and hard to get where he was today, had consistently avoided getting close to anyone.

What if he didn't want to walk away this time?

Pity he'd made a mess of things. Maybe if he devoted half as much time to figuring out what he really wanted with Eve as he had to his pitch he might actually stand a chance at resurrecting the burgeoning relationship he'd botched before it had really begun.

He'd give it a go.

What did he have to lose?

If Eve had to force another brittle smile, her face would crack.

She hated this. Pretending everything was okay with Bryce, having him back to his usual flirty self, putting on a show for her friends while they tossed popcorn at each other and made rude jokes about Mattie and AJ as they did a bit of dirty dancing, bridal waltz style, on the video.

She should be good at acting. It was what she did every day, put on a brave face to hide the insecure mess she was inside.

But tonight was different. She'd reached the end of her tolerance and knew when Bryce dropped her home she'd be struggling not to bawl, or hang onto him, whichever was worse.

'Who's up for another piña colada?'

Mattie held up the jug to a chorus of affirmative cheers while Eve surreptitiously nudged her half-empty glass under the coffee table. That was all she needed, for the alcohol to make her more maudlin.

'You okay?'

Hell, no. She hadn't been okay since she'd first caught sight of his picture on the Internet and was stupid enough to coerce him into dating her to prove a point to her friends.

But she couldn't say that—any of it—with Bryce staring at her with concern.

'I'm fine. Alcohol always makes me sleepy.'

'Well, no more for you, then. We still have another hour or so of making fun of the bride and groom to go yet.'

She forced a smile again, surprised her cheeks didn't seize with the effort.

Leaning closer, he murmured in her ear, 'I know you're not okay. Do you want to leave?'

She shook her head, horrified he'd seen through her act, and bit down on her bottom lip to keep from crying.

'Hey…' He slipped an arm around her waist and cuddled her close, not giving an inch when she initially refused to lean into him. 'You haven't been yourself all evening and I'm betting the last time we met has something to do with that. I promise we'll talk after we leave.'

She didn't want to talk. She'd already tried that and look where it had got her—with him telling her he didn't want to get involved.

No, it was past time for talking. Way past time considering the hollowness deep in her soul, the empty ache because she was missing out on something great.

'Excuse me.' She surged off the floor and made a beeline for the bathroom, needing space to collect her wits before she fell apart.

As she slammed the bathroom door, leaned against it and took great shuddering breaths, she knew it would take a lifetime to get past this feeling, this feeling she daren't name for recognising how monumentally stupid she might've been in falling for a guy like Bryce.

She waited a full five minutes before re-opening the door, only to be confronted by the bridal babes lined up against the opposite wall, arms folded, expressions concerned.

'You ok, hon?'

Mattie rushed forward first, slipping an arm around her waist, while Carol and Linda crowded her from the other side.

'You don't look so good,' Carol said, while Linda merely tut-tutted.

A hand flew over Mattie's mouth. 'You're not...?' She sent a pointed look at her belly.

Eve shrieked, 'No way!'

'Right, guess that settles that.' Linda, the ever pragmatic one, bustled them towards the backdoor. 'Pow-wow. Now.'

Eve loved her friends but talking was the last thing she felt like right now. She wanted to get this evening over and done with, and never have to see Bryce again.

Then why did the thought of watching him walk out of her life send her into an emotional free fall she had no hope of recovering from?

'Something's wrong, hon, and if you don't tell us you know we're going to drag it out of you eventually.'

Mattie's belligerent expression was matched by Carol and Linda and she knew from past experience they wouldn't leave her alone until she gave them something, so she blurted the first and foremost thing in her head.

'I'm in love with Bryce.'

'But that's great!'

Mattie clapped excitedly while Carol and Linda did a little jig.

'It's about time. We'd just about given up on you, what with you burying yourself in work or holing up at home.'

She shook her head, trying not to blame the girls for getting her into this predicament. She might've wanted to avoid being the only single bridesmaid among all their gushing wedded bliss but she'd been the one stupid enough to fall in love with a guy so wrong for her.

Shaking her head, she plopped down onto a garden bench and sagged against it.

'It's not great.'

'Why?'

She waited until the girls sat next to her, jostling for the position closest to her, before she continued her sorry tale.

'I've lied to all of you. Bryce and I aren't dating for real.'

Three mouths dropped open in unison.

'You're always so gung-ho at weddings. Roping me into bridesmaid duties, making sure I don't feel left out. Either that or you're feeling sorry for me and, honestly, I'm tired of being single and I didn't want you worrying about me at Mattie's wedding so I got Bryce to agree to be my date.'

Mattie was the first to close her mouth, only to open it again a second later. 'But this doesn't make any sense. You two are the real deal. Anyone can see that. The way he looks at you, the way you glow around him—how can that be fake?'

Carol laid a hand on Mattie's arm. 'Let her

finish.' Sending her a curious look, she said, 'There's more, isn't there?'

Eve nodded, relaunched into her story.

'Bryce was my brother's best mate in high school. We used to chat a bit back then but I didn't really know him.' Discounting that one amazing night when she thought she had, only to have him walk away regardless. 'We're opposites in every way imaginable and I was the one who stipulated our dating be platonic but...' She trailed off, struck once again by how pathetic she was in falling for him.

'But you went and fell in love for real,' Linda finished, reaching out to rub her back. 'It's okay, sweetie. Why don't you tell him how you feel? I think you'll be verbalising what he's feeling too.'

Shuddering at the thought of having that particular conversation with Bryce after he'd said a resounding no to dating for real, she shook her head.

'Aren't you guys the teensiest bit mad I deceived you?'

To her amazement, they laughed before Mattie leaned forward and chucked her under the chin.

'Hon, we get it. It's hard being single, even harder having your friends fussing over your personal life and making you trudge up the aisle in front of them repeatedly. We just want you to be happy and now you are.'

'But I'm not, I'm miserable.'

'With the potential to be happier than you've ever been if you *talk* to the guy.'

'But he doesn't feel the same way.'

Linda rolled her eyes. 'Trust us on this one, sweet-cakes. He does feel the same way. We've seen his look before—on Anton, Duane and AJ. The guy's not only smitten with you, he's head over heels.'

Fear, potent and consuming, churned in her gut. She'd already tried talking to Bryce and look where that had got her: with a swift *thanks, but no thanks.*

He simply wasn't interested in her that way and everything that had happened between them had either been an act for the benefit of her friends or a spur of the moment thing. What guy wouldn't say no to a girl who was practically draped all over him and, sadly, that was how she must've come across: desperate and dateless. She shuddered and swiped a hand across her eyes.

'Hon, you have to do this. Otherwise, you may lose out on the best thing that ever happened to you.'

Tired of talking, exhausted down to her bones, Eve knew she'd have to agree to get the girls to leave her alone. Right now, she wanted to head home, relax and wallow in her misery. If that happened to involve drowning her sorrows in a litre tub of cherry ice cream, all the better.

Standing, she brushed off her skirt. 'Thanks for the advice, and for being so understanding. I think it's time I headed home and did something about this.'

Like delete Bryce's number from her phone's auto dial.

Mattie jumped to her feet and clapped her hands. 'That's the way. Tackle these guys head-on. Trust me, they don't know what hits them.'

Linda and Carol chuckled and, as the girls headed back inside, Eve knew there'd be no tackling Bryce.

About anything.

'Man, have you got it bad.'

Bryce wrenched his attention away from the window and back to AJ, passing another round of beers to the guys.

'Sorry, what did you say?'

Duane sniggered and Anton placed a thumb in the middle of his forehead.

'Mate, she's got you under her thumb already and you aren't even hitched yet. Let me tell you, it only gets worse from here.'

Bryce darted another quick glance out of the window. 'I'm worried about her.'

AJ nodded and raised his beer in his direction. 'See? Smitten.'

Duane toasted him too. 'Yeah, Eve's not in the room for a few minutes and you can't stop looking out for her.'

'But she bolted out of here like there's something seriously wrong.' And he had an awful sinking feeling he knew why.

Duane slung an arm around his shoulders. 'Listen, mate. I'm going to give you some free advice. Women are impossible to understand so there's no use even trying. And once you fall for them it gets a hundred times worse. So chill out. Go with the flow. Whatever's bugging her, she'll tell you soon enough. Trust me, she'll spend hours telling you, going on and on and on...'

The guys laughed while Bryce knew he'd blown it. Something he hoped to change later tonight. He'd give it his best shot; a small part of him hoped she wouldn't be acting this way unless she cared.

Anton's speculative look held a hint of steel beneath. 'Just make sure you treat her right. Eve's had it tough.'

He didn't want to talk about her like this, not with a bunch of guys he'd only recently met. He didn't know what galled him more: the fact these guys knew her better than he did or the fact he wanted to glean as much info from them about her as he could.

'How tough?'

'Carol said Eve's dad died when she was eighteen and she lost the family home. Then her brother ups and leaves for overseas a few years later and she's been on her own ever since. She works damn hard, rarely dates, likes her solitude.'

AJ scratched his head, crinkling his forehead. 'Come to think of it, you're the first guy we've ever seen her date.'

Duane chuckled. 'Yeah, so there's no pressure on you or anything.'

Anton and AJ joined in. 'And don't forget you have to answer to us if you muck her around.'

These guys genuinely cared about Eve and it warmed his heart. He'd already judged them to be good guys and seeing how much they cared about her raised them in his esteem more.

Plonking his beer down on the table, he stood

up. 'Thanks, guys, but I have no intention of mucking Eve around. She's too special for that.'

He strode towards the door amid catcalls and wolf whistles, determined to tell her. However, he didn't get five steps before his mobile rang and, fishing it out of his pocket, he groaned when he saw Sol's number on call display.

'Work,' he mouthed to the guys before heading into the kitchen to take the call.

'Hey, Sol, what's up?'

'I need you to come into the office now. There's a potential glitch in the Hot Pursuit contract I want ironed out ASAP.'

As he watched Eve stroll across the backyard towards the house, soft and pretty and ethereal in the moonlight, the words, *Can't it wait till morning?* died on his lips.

The sooner he took care of business, the sooner he could be back at her place discussing their future.

'No worries, Sol. I'll be there in half an hour.'

'Good. See you then.'

Sol rang off and Bryce thrust the phone back into his pocket and headed for the door.

He had some serious business to take care of…once he'd ironed out the contract.

CHAPTER THIRTEEN

Eve found a shady patch of lawn and curled her feet under her, flipping open the pages of the latest spy novel.

She needed to take her mind off things, namely the fact that Bryce had said he'd drop by last night after he'd taken care of some urgent business at the office.

He'd wanted to talk. She was still waiting.

He'd sent her a text message around midnight saying he was caught up at the office and wouldn't make it and, rather than being disappointed, she'd been relieved. She didn't want him turning up at her home any more, not now.

Their deal was done.

He'd acted as her date, she'd acted like a love-starved fool and fallen for him and, rather than talk about it as the girls suggested, all she wanted to do was put the whole sorry month behind her.

She'd been crazy to concoct the scheme in the first place, though it *had* meant she hadn't been the only single bridesmaid at the wedding for once, and it *had* been fun hanging out with him, *had* been beyond flattering being charmed by him…

Shaking her head, she forced herself to concentrate on the book. Thinking like that would be self-defeating and if there was one thing she'd learned the hard way it was to think positive.

A confirmed optimist, that was her: which explained why a small part of her couldn't help but hope when Bryce had mentioned he wanted to talk, he'd meant about them.

Forget about him.

Easy for her voice of reason to say; the rest of her was having a hard time catching up.

Lifting the book in front of her face, she leaned back against the maple tree, its rigid trunk a solid comfort behind her back. She loved sitting out here on a fine day, lulled by the buzz of bees going about their business as they flitted through her flowers, tuning out the hazy traffic noise of nearby Chapel Street and Toorak Road.

This was what she could depend on, not some hotshot exec who thought nothing of dating a woman he barely knew to advance his own career.

Determinedly ignoring how unfair that was, she buried her nose deeper in her book, reading the same paragraph for the third time.

Bryce found Eve this way, her long bare legs stretched out in front of her, a pair of rimless glasses sliding down her nose and her hair in a sexy, mussed, just-out-of-bed mess.

With her frayed cut-off denim shorts and baggy red T-shirt, she looked cute and rumpled and at one with her surroundings, making him feel like an intruder. Hopefully, he wouldn't feel that way once she heard what he had to say.

Clearing his throat, he took a few steps towards her but she didn't look up, engrossed in the latest spy novel he'd heard about but hadn't had time to read yet.

It wasn't until his shadow fell across her pages did she glance up, her mouth falling open as she leaped to her feet.

'What are you doing here?' she yelled, and his welcoming smile died on his lips as he registered her horrified expression.

'Your line was busy when I called so I left you a message on your mobile. Didn't you get it?'

'Do you think I'd be looking like this if I did?'

Her hands flapped between trying to smooth her hair and tug down the hem of her shorts, adding to her air of delightful dishevelment.

'You look fine.'

He breached the short distance between them to reach out and pluck a piece of bark off her T-shirt but, to his amazement, she shrank back and held up her hands to ward him off.

'I'm a mess. You can't see me like this!'

Dropping his hand, he thrust it into his pocket, at a total loss. Why was she freaking out like this?

'What's wrong?'

'You. Being here. Dropping in unannounced.'

Her choppy words were punctuated by short breaths as her hands resumed their fidgeting and it took all his willpower not to reach out and stop them.

'It's no big deal. It's not like we're strangers, right?'

Hurt flickered in her eyes and for the life of him he couldn't figure out what he'd said wrong this time.

'This isn't a good time for me.'

Yeah, she looked like she was super-busy, but he kept that to himself. Sarcasm would only fuel her fire at the moment, whatever had lit it.

'I'm sorry I didn't make it back last night but I need to talk to you, which is why I'm here.'

She looked straight past him, her gaze darting around as if searching for the quickest escape route.

'I'm not leaving till we talk.'

Her wary stare swung back to him, her frantic hands finally stilling as she pushed her glasses up her nose before folding her arms.

'There's really nothing left to say, is there? You don't need to act as my date any more and I'm sure you've got plenty of work to do, so—'

'I know I've been sending you mixed messages but that's why I'm here, to sort it out. Why are you acting like this?'

He couldn't bear her cold indifference a second longer and stepped into the shade, taking hold of her upper arms, hating it when she stiffened.

Her bottom lip wobbled and he almost bundled her into his arms but he needed to find out what had caused her funk, move past it and concentrate on their future. Together.

'Eve, please, talk to me.'

For a split second her gaze warmed to melted treacle before her lips thinned and she tossed her hair back as if it was immaculately coiffed rather than resembling a bird's nest.

'You can drop the charm act.'

Shrugging out of his grasp, she backed away, stopping short when she bumped into the rose arbour at her back.

'See this?'

Her hands resumed their butterfly impersonation, flapping and flitting all over the place. 'No make-up. Frizzy hair. Glasses. Comfy clothes. This is the real me.'

Her shoulders drooped ever so slightly but the fire in her eyes didn't dim one iota.

'Still the same girl underneath all the trappings. Go ahead, look, really take a good, long, hard look.' She did a bizarre little twirl as he finally twigged what this was all about. 'See? No designer clothes. No sleek hair. No contact lenses. Just plain old Eve, the girl you used to know. Not too impressive, huh?'

'Eve, you're beautiful.'

He knew he'd said the wrong thing the moment the words left his mouth for she straightened, sending him a withering glance that spoke volumes.

'You've got what you wanted out of this so there's no need to pretend any more.'

'I'm not!'

Deriving little satisfaction from her shocked

expression, he lowered his voice with effort and took a deep breath. 'I'm here because I care about you. You, not the clothes you wear or how neat your hair is. Surely you know that?'

Her eyes narrowed, cool, assessing, finding him lacking when she shook her head. 'How would I?'

His heart sinking, he opened his mouth to convince her but she held up a silencing hand.

'For a while there I would've given anything to hear you say that, but not any more.'

'Why?'

'Because I can't compete with your first love.'

His confusion must've shown because she continued, 'Your work. It'll always come first.'

He opened his mouth to protest and she leapt in again.

'You can't deny it. Every time we've grown closer over the last month you've chosen your precious career over exploring what we may've started.'

Waving towards the gate, effectively dismissing him, she continued, 'We're too different, you and I. Your job is the most important thing in your life; for me, it's this place. Being able to unwind at the end of a long day, home-cooked meals, quiet time. For you, I don't think it would ever be enough.'

She tilted her chin up, challenging him to correct her. 'Go on, tell me I'm wrong.'

What could he say? He did thrive on the buzz of business: the networking, the social dinners and drinks, the party schmoozing.

So they were opposites? Big deal. Her cool, unflappable personality intrigued him, was a balm to his outgoing gregariousness. They could make this work, he had no doubts.

'Guilty as charged on the work thing but ever heard of opposites attracting?'

With a resigned shake of her head, she leaned back against the arbour. 'Tell me what you do in your spare time.'

'What?'

'Go ahead, tell me.'

'I play golf, the occasional game of tennis, ski in the winter.'

'Alone?'

'No, usually with work colleagues or clients…' He trailed off, seeing where she was going with this.

'Want to know what I do? I volunteer at the RSPCA. Riveting stuff for a guy like you.'

Figured. She had always used to rescue wounded birds and animals as a kid, another reason he'd steered well clear of her at school back then, not wanting to be treated as another one of her strays if she'd discovered the truth.

Holding his hands out to her palm up, he kept his tone cool, controlled.

'None of this stuff matters. We're individuals; none of that has to change. We'd only be dating, for goodness' sake.'

The instant the fire in her eyes blanked and her expression shut down, he knew he'd said the wrong thing again.

'Eve, honey, we can work this out.'

His mobile rang and he muttered a curse, wishing he'd remembered to turn it off.

Sending a pointed look at his pocket, she said

in a saccharine sweet voice, 'Hadn't you better answer that?'

'No, look—'

'But it could be important. More valuable business?'

With their relationship hanging in the balance, he was inclined to say business be damned but Sol had been riding his case last night, hassling him over every little thing with the Hot Pursuit contract.

He couldn't afford to mess up with that, no matter how much he wanted her. Perhaps he could sneak a peek at the caller ID… No, this was too important. *Eve* was too important.

His hesitation cost him dearly. He could see it in the derisive curl of her upper lip, the disappointment in her eyes.

'You know something? I pity you. Even now, when we're trying to have a heart-to-heart here, you can't tune out from work.'

Only three little words resonated out of her speech.

I pity you.

No one pitied him.

Ever.

He'd had a gutful of it growing up and he sure as hell didn't need the woman he loved pitying him now.

Loved? *Loved?*

Damn, he'd always had lousy timing and it looked as if this was no exception. What a dumb time for him to realise he'd fallen in love with her, when he had no option but to walk away.

Ignoring the unusual ache in the region of his heart, he thrust his hands in his pockets. Ironically, his phone stopped ringing the moment he touched it.

'You're right. I can't. Goodbye, Eve.'

With that, he swivelled on his heel and stalked across the garden, oblivious to the beauty of dahlias and hyacinths and chrysanthemums clambering for space in her beautifully wild garden, dappled sunlight and the warmth of a perfect spring day.

He'd just laid his heart on the line.

And lost.

* * *

Eve watched Bryce stomp off, her heart splintering into itty-bitty pieces.

She'd wanted to drive him away, had done a mighty fine job of it, but she'd never expected to see genuine hurt as she'd flung her final comment at him.

He'd looked devastated, as if her opinion really mattered to him and, rather than being glad he'd gone, it took every ounce of willpower not to run after him and apologise.

She'd overreacted. Big time. Glancing down at her oldest denim shorts and awful shapeless red-faded-to-pink T-shirt, she wrinkled her nose and sank onto the grass, resting her folded arms on her knees, her chin atop them.

No one ever saw her like this—ever—and the last man she wanted to see her so dishevelled was Bryce. She'd seen him checking her out and, while he hadn't run screaming from her yard in horror, there was no way he could be attracted to someone like her.

'You're beautiful.'

She squeezed her eyes shut, blotting out the

memory of him saying those words with a tender expression in his eyes.

Was the guy blind? Delusional? Both? She looked like a fright and he'd paid her a compliment like that?

What if he'd meant it? What if she was letting the same old insecurities ruin any chance of happiness she could have with the love of her life?

Her eyes flew open as the impact of her thoughts struck her anew.

The love of her life.

Bryce was the love of her life.

Oh, heck.

Leaping off the grass, she dusted off her butt and raced towards the house. However, as she neared the back door and heard him gun the engine of his Aston Martin, her steps slowed.

What was she going to do—accost him after booting him out of the door? No, better to give him some time to cool down, get herself tidied up and then work out what she was going to say.

For she had absolutely no doubt when she spoke to him next, it would be the most important speech of her life.

CHAPTER FOURTEEN

HE'D failed.

Him, the guy who never, ever let the F word enter his head, let alone his vocabulary, had failed spectacularly with Eve.

And he hated it.

She may have acted like a crazy person when he'd showed up at her place but he'd overreacted too, stomping out like a sulky brat.

Now he'd had time to think, he knew what he had to do. He'd never failed at business, he'd be damned if he sat back and let his relationship with Eve fail before it had really begun.

She was right. He always put business first, always had. He'd never questioned why, never had any reason to. Until now. Falling in love, potentially losing that love, had him doing some serious soul-searching and, as much as it pained him, he had to face up to a few home truths.

He'd finally figured out why business was everything, why his drive to succeed went above and beyond rational human emotion.

He had to tell Eve all of it if they were to have any chance.

Now this.

When he'd landed the Hot Pursuit campaign, he had no idea he'd be based in Sydney for a good part of the next year.

It was an opportunity too good to pass up, an opportunity he'd worked his ass off for. But if they couldn't maintain a fake relationship in the same city, what hope did he have of convincing her to give a real relationship a shot, long distance?

Sitting on a plane bound for the Harbour city to start the ball rolling had given him plenty of time to think, time to plan…

When he returned, they'd have that chat he'd wanted yesterday.

This time, he wouldn't settle for anything less than gut-wrenching honesty from both of them.

* * *

He'd upped and gone to Sydney.

Just like that.

Leaving her aching and depressed and heart-broken.

She couldn't concentrate at work, couldn't face her friends and couldn't be bothered entering her kitchen, a sure sign she was in a bad, bad way.

Only one way to deal with this—head-on—and, thankfully, some creepy colleague named Davin had let her into Bryce's office, saying it was okay to leave a note.

She sank into Bryce's chair behind his desk and reached for a pen. Her plan was to leave him a note so he wouldn't have the option of not answering her call, a likely proposition after she'd behaved like a shrieking shrew yesterday.

The memory alone made her cringe and, grabbing a pen, she found a notepad tucked under a stack of paperwork. Tapping the end of the pen against her bottom lip, she searched for the right words, mentally rehearsing a few different versions of what she wanted to say before deleting them all.

'Well, isn't this just peachy,' she muttered, the pen rapping faster and faster as she racked her brain to come up with something that didn't sound pathetic or desperate or an embarrassing combination of the two.

Her gaze drifted to the notepad, idly scanned the scribble, seeing it without actually reading it.

The squiggles soon coalesced, yet she still couldn't make sense of it and she peered closer, intrigued by the precise documentation of digital times in the left-hand column with a printed jumble of words in the right, like some kind of weird shorthand.

Probably some weird ad-world-speak and, annoyed she'd become distracted, she flipped the top page and started writing 'Dear Bryce'.

She still had no idea what she was going to say but, as the words dribbled out, she knew one thing. She owed him an apology *and* an explanation and, if he didn't respond to her note, she'd camp out on his doorstep to get him to hear her out.

He'd walked away from her once without an

explanation. She'd be damned if she stood by and let him do it again.

Eve had just baked her last batch of double choc fudge brownies when the phone rang.

Wiping her hands on a dishcloth, and trying not to notice the staggering array of comfort baking on the benchtop, she answered.

'Eve, it's Bryce.'

Her heart soared as she sagged against the doorway in relief that he'd called. 'How are you?'

'Just back from Sydney, got your note.'

'Good.'

'I'd like to see you.'

He paused, as if weighing up his next words. 'Which is why I'm ringing first, of course.'

She heard the wary amusement in his tone and she couldn't help but laugh. 'Smart guy, considering my little performance the last time you dropped by. I'd like to see you too. Are you too tired to pop over now? I've baked brownies.'

'Sounds good.'

'And apple pie. And lemon tart. And a mountain of shortbread.'

His deep chuckles washed over her, low and sexy. 'Lucky I didn't eat much on the plane. I'll be there in fifteen minutes.'

'Great.'

There was so much she wanted to say, starting with *I'm sorry* and ending with *I love you.*

She settled for, 'I'm really looking forward to seeing you.'

'Same here, sweetheart.'

She rang off on a sigh, clutching the phone to her chest, his endearment reaching down to the lonely place in her soul and filling it with blossoming warmth.

Fifteen minutes.

Her gaze instantly flew to the glass cabinet opposite, seeing her reflection in all its mussed glory. She had loads of time to make herself presentable, yet, as she swivelled towards the hallway leading to her bedroom, her steps faltered.

What happened to being completely honest with him? Was a trowel-load of make-up, blow-dried hair and a designer outfit the real her?

Uh-uh. He was coming to see her and, for once, she was going to let him see the real her, without qualms, without reservations. It would make her admission all the more sincere, would put her old insecurities to rest, once and for all.

She'd been terrified he'd bolt if he saw the real her without all the trappings, the same way he'd bolted eight years ago, yet he was coming over despite seeing her at her worst that day in the garden.

Probably to tell her she was loony, but hey, he was making the effort and the least she could do was keep an open mind. She'd desperately wanted this opportunity, now all she had to do was not mess it up.

Casting one last longing look in the direction of her bedroom, where a plethora of beauty parapher-nalia and designer outfits awaited her, she deliber-ately turned her back and returned to the benchtop.

Icing cupcakes would keep her hands busy and her mind off the terrifying thought that, despite everything she planned on saying to Bryce, he could still walk out her door and never look back.

* * *

Bryce had never been scared of anything.

He'd learned early on to face his fears, grapple and conquer them. It was how he'd survived school, how he'd gone back and got his high school diploma, how he'd got to where he was in the advertising world today.

Yet, right now, standing on Eve's doorstep clutching a bunch of her favourite violets with a very important document tucked into his jacket pocket, he had to admit to a certain amount of trepidation.

He'd come here to tell her the truth.

Would she think less of him? Would she pity him? Or, worse, would she open her heart to the possibility of them having a relationship because she considered him one of her strays who needed mollycoddling and nurturing?

He couldn't stand any of those options but he had to give it to her straight if they were to have any chance at the future he so desperately wanted.

As he raised his hand to knock again, the door swung open and he smiled, a purely instinctive response to the fresh, vibrant woman standing before him with a flour smudge on her nose and chocolate streaking her right cheek.

'Thanks for coming,' she said, holding the door open, her eyes lighting up when she spied the violets he brought out from behind his back.

'These are for you.'

'Thanks.'

She buried her nose in them, her gently mussed hair draping over the soft purple petals in a beautiful contrast of dark chocolate against deep amethyst.

He loved her hair like this, loose and curling, with that 'just out of bed' look rather than sleek and styled to within an inch of its life like she usually wore it.

Straightening, she caressed one of the petals, her genuine smile shooting straight to his heart.

'Come on in. There's a bakery's worth of cakes and pastries awaiting you.'

'Sounds great.'

He fell into step beside her, following the delicious trail of apples and cinnamon and vanilla permeating the air.

'And smells even better.'

'I think I went overboard.'

She waved towards the benchtop, and the table, and the stove. Every conceivable surface was covered in a staggering array of mouth-watering delicacies and, while his stomach grumbled accordingly, all he could think about was how much he'd like to taste the chocolate smearing her cheek.

'You like baking. Nothing wrong with that.'

'I cook when I'm nervous.'

Her gaze flickered to his and what he saw there shocked the hell out of him.

Fear.

She was as scared as he was.

Hoping his smile reassured her, he brushed his thumb against her cheek.

'Chocolate smudge,' he said when she raised an eyebrow. 'And flour here.' He tweaked her nose and she laughed, the sound warm and familiar. 'So why are you nervous?'

'The million dollar question.'

Cradling her violets like a precious bundle, she headed for the sink, rummaging for a vase underneath and giving him ample opportunity to study her.

Apart from the afternoon he'd surprised her in the backyard when she'd gone crazy, he'd never seen her so casual: worn denim jeans frayed at the cuffs, plain white singlet top and flip-flops.

He liked it, liked the fact she felt comfortable enough around him now not to get all tizzed up. In fact, the more he thought about, he realised he'd never seen her looking anything other than immaculate.

Personally, he liked looking good. His job demanded it, but there was nothing like kicking back in jeans and a T-shirt on the weekends with a healthy three-day growth.

'Are you going to answer the question?'

Sending him a wry grin, she stood and filled a cut glass vase with water. 'How much time have you got?'

'All the time in the world.'

Crossing to the breakfast bar, he pulled out a stool and sat. 'Besides, the sooner we chat, the sooner I get to devour all this.'

Her chuckle sounded forced, nervous as she busied herself unwrapping the violets and arranging them in the vase as if she were auditioning for florist of the year.

'The flowers can wait.'

He reached across the bench separating them and laid a hand on her forearm, not surprised it gave a little tremor.

Yeah, she was as nervous as he was, but he'd be damned if he backed down now. She had to hear what he had to say.

All of it.

With a long heartfelt sigh, she placed the vase on the windowsill and nodded. 'You're right. Guess I'm just not sure where to start.'

'Don't tell me you've got some deep dark secret to unburden too?'

He'd meant it as a joke, a bit of light-hearted banter to get the ball rolling. Instead, her eyes clouded with pain and a faint blush stained her cheeks.

'Hey, I was kidding.'

She gnawed on her bottom lip, twisting a

strand of hair around her index finger. 'Why don't you go first?'

'Okay, but maybe you should sit down.'

'That bad, huh?'

'Depends on your definition of bad.'

Once again, his attempt at humour fell flat as a tiny crease appeared between her brows and it was then it struck him.

She was wearing glasses again. Funny how it hadn't registered at first, but then, it was all she used to wear in high school and, while this new rimless variety was more trendy than the thick plastic frames she used to wear, they seemed a part of her, a part of the girl he knew and liked and respected, despite acting like a jerk whenever they crossed paths.

'Let's go through to the lounge room and make ourselves comfortable. Fancy a drink?'

He shook his head. 'Thanks, but I'd rather just talk.'

'Suit yourself.'

She preceded him into the lounge room and it took all his willpower not to reach out and touch her softly curling hair swinging over her shoulders to see if it felt as silky as it looked.

He deliberately waited until she chose a seat, doing an inner high-five when she sat on the three-seat sofa and he sat next to her. To her credit, she didn't scoot away or flinch but he saw the wariness in her eyes, the tension around her mouth.

And that was before he started his spiel.

Leaning back, the document in his pocket gave a noisy crackle, as if reminding him there was no better place to start than the beginning.

Slipping his hand into his pocket, he drew it out, tapping it against his thigh, searching for the right words before deciding to jump straight in.

'I'd planned on telling you the truth that night I was going to come by but never made it because of work. And then things got botched when I dropped around that afternoon you weren't expecting me. But there's something you need to know before I explain why I went to Sydney and what it has to do with us.'

Flipping the document between his fingers, he clenched his fingers around it before holding it out. 'Here. I think you should take a look at this. It might make things clearer.'

Her puzzled frown intensified as she unfolded the paper and read it, the tip of her tongue protruding as she moved down the page at a speed he'd never hope to match. Reading wasn't his forte. Along with spelling, writing and telling the time.

Confusion creased her brow as she rattled the paper in her hand. 'What's this?'

'Remember that book report on *Pride and Prejudice* we had to submit to pass English Lit in Year Ten?'

'Uh-huh.'

'That's mine.'

Her gaze dropped to the page again before raising to meet his, a thousand questions visible in the dark depths he'd gladly drown in.

'But—'

'It's a mess, I know.'

Taking it from her, he stared at the document that had spurred him on to get where he was today, the document with a big fat F in the top right-hand corner, the document that had effectively ended his chance of passing high school but had eventually changed his life.

Running his index finger down the page, he stared at the muddle, knowing he could almost recite the thing word for word; he'd looked at it often enough over the years. 'The b's and d's are transposed. Simple words like saw and was are confused. Words are spelled how they sound, like duz for does, pleeze for please, nock for knock, serch for search and jerney for journey. Not pretty, is it?'

Comprehension dawned as her puzzled frown disappeared. 'The lists, your note-taking, the software you wouldn't let me see, that weird shorthand I saw on your desk and this.' She stabbed at the paper. 'You're dyslexic.'

Nodding, he folded it and tossed it onto the table in front of them.

'Diagnosed courtesy of that particular masterpiece. Much too late, mind you, considering I'd failed almost everything at school by then.'

Laying a hand on his arm, she leaned closer, her soft vanilla scent enveloping him in a comforting cloud. 'I have no idea what you went through at school because of it, but look how far you've come in your career. You're at the top of your game and that's great.'

He scanned her face for the slightest hint of pity but all he saw was genuine admiration.

'Thanks. Funnily enough, while I can't spell or read or write real well, apparently I'm highly intuitive and insightful, think in pictures instead of words, have a vivid imagination, think and perceive multi-dimensionally and can use my brain to alter and create perceptions.'

Forcing a chuckle, he laid a hand over hers. 'How's that for a diagnosis?'

Her grip tightened on his arm. 'When did they discover it?'

'After I'd left school. I was throwing out a heap of junk and our neighbour who'd come over to take an old stereo saw this, asked me how I'd coped at school because his nephew was dyslexic too.'

'The teachers never picked it up?'

'The teachers just thought I was a screw-up, along with my folks.'

He could see the pity hovering in her eyes, an apology for what he'd gone through hovering on her lips and he rushed on. 'But, thanks to that guy, I discovered what I was dealing with, sought advice from experts, learned to deal with it, got my high school diploma and didn't look back.'

'That's fantastic. You should be really proud of yourself.'

'I am, but not about how I treated you because of it.'

Her eyebrows shot up. 'Me?'

Nodding, he captured both her hands in his, empowered by the understanding on her face.

'Tony's party, why I acted like a jerk at the end?'

'Uh-huh.'

'It was because of this.'

He jerked his head in the direction of the paper. 'I knew there was something wrong all through school. I didn't learn like the other kids, felt stupid because of it.'

A tiny indentation creased her brow and it took all his willpower not to lean over and kiss it away with his lips.

'We connected that night; why did you walk away?'

Squeezing her hands, he released them, dragged a nervous hand through his hair.

'Until that night, I was doing fine as long as I swaggered around pretending I was cool, making wisecracks rather than knuckling down. It was why I teased you at home, avoided you at school, because I thought someone as smart as you would see right through me.'

He shrugged, knowing his reasoning sounded trite now, feeling every kind of fool. 'That night we clicked? We hadn't seen each other in a few years, I'd always thought you were cute but aloof; yet when I strutted up to you, ready to be rebuffed when I teased, your eyes sparkled. You didn't look away or focus on the buttons on my shirt, you looked at me, really looked at me and, before I knew it, we were talking. Really talking, like I'd never talked to anyone in my life.'

She gnawed at her bottom lip, a thoughtful action that had no right being erotic.

'So it wasn't about my looks?'

Confused, he shook his head. 'Why would you think that?'

With a wry grin, she pointed at her glasses.

'The fact I wore these. And wore my hair in plaits rather than bobbed like the other girls. And had the daggiest wardrobe on the planet.'

'I didn't see any of that.'

Eve's heart swelled with joy as she scanned Bryce's face for the slightest hint he wasn't telling the truth, daring to believe when all she saw was his bright blue eyes gleaming with sincerity.

'Then what did you see?'

Her pulse stuttered and she held her breath as he reached out, trailing his fingertips over her cheek as if memorising every dip, every curve.

'I saw an amazing girl who loved her brother and her dad, who adored wounded animals, who wanted to be the best she could be by applying herself hard. I saw a cute, intelligent girl who actually looked at me like I had something interesting to say, a girl who could make me laugh with her quick words, a shy girl transforming into an intriguing woman.'

'Yet you still walked.'

He grimaced. 'You left out the part about laughing at you.'

She blinked, the flicker of hurt in her eyes slugging him hard. 'Remember what we were talking about before I almost kissed you?'

Remember? She remembered every tiny detail about that night, despite all attempts to forget.

She nodded. 'Our dreams for the future.'

'That's right. I was so caught up in our conversation, I almost spilled my guts and I couldn't let that happen. At that time, with your brains, you were always going to be successful while I thought I was stupid and didn't know why.'

Her heart flipped, realising what he'd been through, and she reached out to him, covered his lips with her fingers. 'It's okay, you don't have to—'

'I want to; let me finish.' He captured her hand, lowered it. 'When you were talking about your dreams for the future, I'd never seen anything so beautiful. You glowed, your face was alive and I had to kiss you. Then those jerks interrupted and I had a reality check. In a few hours, I'd let you get closer than anyone and it scared the hell out of me. I couldn't offer you anything, I was a nobody and you were chasing a dream. I had to push you away.'

He shook his head, his smile wry. 'So I laughed along with those guys, pretended what we'd shared meant nothing, and walked away.'

Stunned, she assimilated the truth, silently berating herself for believing the worst all these years, thanks to her own insecurities, focused on the one thing he'd said that she couldn't forget.

'You thought I was cute? I glowed? But I was a geek.'

His hand slid around to cradle her head while he leaned closer, his lips hovering near her ear.

'An adorable geek.'

Her breath caught as he brushed the softest kiss on her cheek, a barely-there movement reminiscent of the flimsiest flutter of butterfly wings against her skin.

She tilted her head to the right ever so slightly, rewarded by a groan as he captured her mouth in a feverish kiss, a hot, raw melding of lips that sent ecstasy spiralling out of control through her.

Shivers of delight ran down her spine as his mouth grazed hers hungrily, repeatedly, his tongue tracing the contours of her lips, dipping into the recesses of her mouth, searching, ravaging, searing a path directly to her soul.

When he kissed her like this, she felt beautiful and treasured and special, rendering her old insecurities irrelevant. When he kissed her like this, she could almost believe that, for one magical moment, they had a chance.

But they didn't. No matter what he'd said, no matter how badly she wanted a relationship, he still wasn't the guy for her. How could he be, when he'd flit off to whichever end of the earth his precious career took him?

He stilled and pulled away, cradling her face in his hands, his eyes shining with passion.

'What's wrong?'

She had to tell him the truth.

It was what tonight was all about but, now the

moment had arrived, her gut churned with nerves and her palms grew clammy.

Truth was nice in theory, in the wee small hours of the morning, alone with her thoughts. Putting it into practice with the guy she'd fallen in love with staring at her with tenderness was the pits.

'Don't you want to know why I acted like a crazy person when you dropped by unannounced?'

A soft smile curved his lips. 'Does it matter?'

Oh, yeah. He needed to know why; he needed to know all of it.

'Eve?'

Blinking, she reached up to his hands and disengaged them from her face. She couldn't think, let alone speak with him touching her, no matter how incredible it felt.

'This is the real me.'

He raised an eyebrow, following her hands as she waved them up and down. 'I know.'

'I'm not glamorous. Or elegant. Or super-cool.'

His mouth kicked into a smile. 'Considering

some of those sexy suits you wear to work, I beg to differ.'

Her heart sinking, she shook her head. 'Those clothes, the make-up, the blow-dried hair, are all an illusion. A confidence mask I need to step out that door and face the world.'

His smile faded as he absorbed the impact of her words. 'But you're brilliant. And gorgeous. Why would you need any sort of mask?'

Sinking back into the sofa, she covered her face with her hands. How could she explain without sounding like a freak?

'Eve, tell me.'

He gently pried her hands free, his forehead creased with concern.

'This is going to sound ridiculous.'

'Try me.'

He hadn't released her hands and, for a moment, she was grateful. Having him hold her steady, infusing her with solid warmth, was beyond comforting.

Taking a deep breath, she tightened her grip on his hands. 'My new image? The clothes, the make-up, the hair? Courtesy of you.'

He frowned. 'I don't follow.'

'Tony's party was the first night I wore a dress, lipstick, contacts. And you noticed me, treated me like a woman and it felt great.'

'Then I walked. Some guy.'

She hoped her gentle smile went some way to erasing the bitterness lacing his words.

'Actually, whether you walked or not, you did me a favour. The time we spent together? Talking, laughing, flirting? I'd never felt that way before. It felt good, damn good, and I wanted to feel that way all the time. And if wearing that stuff made me feel good, got that kind of attention—' she shrugged sheepishly '—I wanted people to look at me like that all the time. So I undertook major makeovers. Chose a career where people would look at me and think how fabulously glamorous I was…'

She trailed off, feeling suddenly foolish.

'And?'

'The woman I've become is not who I am. Despite all the trimmings, I'm still an insecure introvert who's terrified of anyone discovering the truth.'

When his frown deepened, she continued, 'I'm a fraud. I hide behind my business and my clothes and my image, dead scared of anyone getting too close.'

'Why?'

He squeezed her hands gently, encouraging, and she knew she had to tell him everything, despite the urge to clam up.

'Because I lose everyone who gets too close.'

There, she'd said it, enunciated her greatest fear and, rather than badger her or belittle her admission, he released her hands to slide an arm around her shoulder, snuggling her into the protective circle.

'Is this about your dad?'

'Mum, Dad, Tony—all of them.'

'Don't forget me. We got close that night and I walked too.'

She focused on the seam of her jeans and a tiny fray, hating the helpless feeling welling, the same feeling that had swamped her after her dad's death and the extent of her loss had really become apparent.

'You to a lesser degree, but you know Mum died when Tony and I were toddlers so that wasn't as hard to take as Dad dying.'

'There's more, isn't there?'

Sighing, she nodded. 'Dad had so many debts, we lost the family home. Tony and I had nothing. And then Tony up and left a few years later.'

He muttered a curse, cuddling her closer. 'And you were totally alone.'

She nodded, remembering the emptiness, the fear, the grief.

'It's why I've shut myself off, why I don't get too close emotionally to anyone. It's not worth the risk, not worth the pain.'

A fragile silence greeted her pronouncement, stretching into uncomfortable, and she risked a glance at his face. What she saw there took her breath away.

Raw vulnerability, totally at odds with his usual confidence.

'What about me?'

'You?'

Tipping up her chin, he stared into her eyes, mesmerising, compelling. 'Am I worth the risk?'

Confusion clouded her brain. Was he asking what she thought he was asking…? Did he want her to take a chance on him emotionally?

Scanning his face for some clue as to his feelings, she plucked at the frayed seam until he stilled her nervous fingers with his hand.

'You're not the only one who shut off from people. I've done my fair share of hiding.'

She scanned his face, surprised at the pain and regret clouding his eyes. 'Hiding from your dyslexia?'

He shook his head, his remorse intensifying. 'I've never had a relationship. Casual dates, plenty, but I never felt truly confident enough to let a woman get close until I was financially successful.'

'Why?'

'Because I've always seen my dyslexia as a flaw. Crazy, I know, because it's readily diag-nosed these days and kids get the assistance they need much earlier. But I grew up thinking I was dumb and, when I finally discovered the truth, I still saw it as a defect, a failing. Being financially successful would offset an imperfection like that.'

'Nobody's perfect!'

'I know but, considering my parents' frigid marriage, my lack of close emotional intimacy with anyone, I guess it was as good an excuse as any to never get involved emotionally.'

'Oh.'

Guess that put paid to her hopes for a long and meaningful relationship.

'Until now.'

Her dashed hopes leaped, twirled, did a little jig.

'I asked you a few minutes ago if I was worth the risk. Maybe this will make it easier for you to answer.'

His gaze locked on hers, sincere and honest and filled with an emotion that snatched air from her lungs. 'I'm in love with you. I want us to have a real relationship, to develop what we've started over this last month.'

His mouth kicked into a heart-warming grin. 'I want us to create fireworks.'

Her heart seized as numbness at his declaration melted into a comforting warm and fuzzy happiness. She wanted to believe him, to take a chance.

But her self-preservation mechanisms were too ingrained, too entrenched. Losing her dad and Tony had hurt, but nothing in comparison to what she'd go through if she opened her heart completely to Bryce and lost the love of her life.

He'd walked away from her once when she'd got too close—he'd said it—so what would stop him doing it again?

Taking a deep breath, hating what she had to do, she slowly slipped out of his embrace. 'I'm sorry, I can't.'

Striding across the room, she propped herself against the marble fireplace, blinking back tears, willing the sobs bubbling from deep within to subside.

'I'm not going anywhere.'

'It's better you do,' she murmured, clenching the mantelpiece so hard her knuckles stood out.

'I mean in the future.'

She jumped as he placed a hand on her

shoulder, so wrapped up in her misery she hadn't heard him sneak up on her.

Whirling to face him, she shrugged off his hand, needing to end this now before she broke down completely. 'You will. You'll leave as soon as the next big job offer comes your way. Your work defines you. It's who you are.'

He opened his mouth to respond and she held up a hand.

'You said so yourself. And after learning about your dyslexia tonight, I understand. With every step up the career ladder you take, you triumph over your learning disability, over all those who ever doubted you. I get that. I respect you for it. But I won't hand you my heart, only to have it carved up when you jet off in search of the next big opportunity that comes your way.'

Rather than her words antagonising him, he merely thrust his hands in his pockets and rocked back on his heels, his expression patient.

'Why do you think I told you about my dyslexia?'

That flummoxed her.

Now she came to think about it, he didn't have to tell her. How he'd treated her as a teenager had no bearing on the here and now.

'I have no idea.'

Sliding his hands out of his pockets, he held them out to her, palm up, as if he had nothing to hide.

'Because I trust you. I've been doing some serious thinking, figuring out why I'm so hung up on work and I've finally worked out that the harder I strive, the easier it is to ignore I have a problem, something I face and fight every day.'

Her resolve weakened but, before she could respond, he ploughed on.

'I told you because I want you to know what you're getting into with me, faults and all. Because I thought we shared something special over this last month. Because I thought you might feel something for me and, if it's half of what I feel for you, it's worth fighting for.'

The tears that had been threatening for the last few minutes spilled over in an angry torrent, splashing against her glasses, blurring her vision.

'Eve, honey.'

He bundled her in his arms before she could resist and, slipping off her glasses and flinging them onto a nearby chair, she buried her face in his chest and let the tears fall in great gushes, drenching his T-shirt, emptying her soul.

She clutched at him while he soothed her, shushed her, smoothing her hair, her back, gentle soothing strokes that lulled her until she had nothing left to give.

When the last sob subsided, she took a great shuddering breath and pulled away, all too aware of how she must look: blotchy skin, red nose, bloodshot puffy eyes.

Swiping a hand across her eyes, she focused on the damp patch spreading across his chest.

'I must look a fright.'

Tipping her chin up, he said, 'You look like the woman I'm in love with.'

Wrenching out of his grip, she stepped back, the mantelpiece digging into her back.

'I'm not that woman. The last month has been a sham and, after what I've just told you, surely you know I'm not the right woman for you? You're extroverted and outgoing and spontaneous. I'm introverted and shy and private. I'm a homebody, you're a mover and shaker. Stability is everything to me, this place is everything. Your business will always come first—'

'Shh…' He placed a finger against her lips, effectively shutting her up. 'That's another thing I wanted to tell you. I went to Sydney to organise a stand-in for me.'

'Stand-in for what?'

'The Hot Pursuit contract would've had me in Sydney for most of the year.'

'Then what are you doing here?'

'Because my business doesn't always come first. Time to put down some roots and I want to make Melbourne my base.'

'Oh.'

'With you,' he added, in case she hadn't understood that part.

Her resolve wavered. He'd chosen her over his

precious business. Some statement—and proof he must really, truly love her.

Could it be this simple? Despite their differences, despite her insecurities?

Gripped by a strange compulsion to prove her point one last time, she flapped her hands around.

'Look at me. Really look at me and tell me I'm the woman you want.'

Stepping into her personal space, he grasped her upper arms.

'Don't you know me well enough by now? Don't you have any idea what I find most attractive about you? This.'

He placed a hand over her heart, his palm burning her, branding her through the thin cotton of her T-shirt. 'Your warmth. Your compassion. Your vitality. Yes, I think you're hot and yes, I love those sexy little suits you wear, but guess what? In all the time we dated, real or otherwise, you were cutest when all ruffled and flustered in that baggy top and cut-off shorts, with your hair looking like a flock of magpies had nested in it.'

She opened her mouth to protest. The guy had to be certifiable if he thought she looked cute when she was at her worst: which was pretty much how she was at home most of the time.

Before she had a chance to say anything, he held his fingers over her mouth.

'I love you now. I'll love you when you're old and grey and wrinkly and toothless. I'll love you when gravity has done its worst. So how do you feel about that? Think you can handle having me around that long?'

Her heart expanded with love—love for this crazy, spontaneous, fun-loving guy who'd swept into her life and made her feel—really feel—for the first time in for ever.

She'd emotionally shut down after her dad died, after Tony left, and now she had this amazing man offering her the world.

What was she waiting for?

The corners of her mouth twitched as she gently pushed away his hand, intertwining her fingers with his. 'You know, I've heard gravity sucks. You sure you want to stick around that long?'

His loud cheer, complete with victory punch in the air, left her in little doubt as to his true feelings.

'I'm sure,' he said, a second before his lips crushed hers in a breath-stealing, toe-curling kiss that left her weak-kneed and trembling and wanting him more than ever.

Smiling against his mouth, she braced her palms against his chest, relishing the rock-hard muscles beneath, eager to explore what she could quite smugly term as hers now.

'Old and wrinkly?'

He nodded, his slow, sexy smile warming her better than the chocolate brownies she'd devoured in a fit of nerves before he'd arrived.

'Yeah, I'll still be around when you're ancient and creased and crinkled all over.'

Laughing, she slid her palms upwards and slung her hands around his neck, toying with the soft hair at his nape.

'Grey and toothless too?'

'Oh, yeah, you can't get rid of me, even when you're a fully fledged member of the blue-rinse brigade and your falsies are in a cup next to mine on the bed stand.'

'How romantic!'

He joined in her laughter, his eyes warm and glowing, radiating a love she'd never dreamed possible while his hands slowly strummed her back, strong and sure and tantalising.

'We're the real deal, Eve.'

'No more deals.'

She stood on tiptoe and pressed a tender, tantalising kiss against his lips. 'Unless you count the one where I intend to make an honest man out of you.'

He groaned and leaned his forehead against hers. 'Let me guess. You want to become a bridal babe.'

Despite his flippancy, her heart clenched with the impact of committing to this man for the rest of her life.

'I do.'

She cupped his cheek and stared into the clear blue eyes she could quite happily spend a lifetime looking into.

Wearing the goofy grin of a guy who'd had all his dreams come true, he picked her up, spun her around until she was dizzy and giggling, finally halting and sliding her down in delicious full frontal contact.

'I guess Eve Gibson has a nice ring to it,' he said, nuzzling her neck until she squealed.

'Is that a proposal?'

Her breath caught as he nipped the sensitive skin above her collarbone, sending shivers of longing racing through her body.

'You bet. How soon do you want to become a bridal babe?'

Her, a bride? Surreal. When she'd devised her crazy plan to not be the last single bridesmaid at Mattie's wedding, little had she known how far she'd go to stay off it permanently!

'Soon, my love, soon. How about we date for a while so you get to see me like this all the time? For now, there's a kitchen full of goodies that need to be eaten and I've heard the way to a man's heart is through his stomach.'

Capturing her hand, he placed it against his heart, where it beat strong and solid beneath her palm.

'My heart's already all yours. For always.'

As his mouth brushed hers in a sweet lingering kiss, Eve had never felt so secure, so cherished, so loved.

Bryce was her present, her future, her dream.

And she had no intention of waking up any time soon.

EPILOGUE

'SWEETIE, the caterers want to know if it's time to serve dessert.'

Eve dragged her starry-eyed gaze away from her husband, talking to AJ on the periphery of the dance floor, and turned to Mattie. 'Sure, tell them to lay everything out on the buffet table, let people help themselves.'

Mattie shook her head. 'I can't believe you did all this.'

Eve shrugged. 'It's what I do.'

'For a job! You should've let someone else organise your wedding.'

'Bryce and I wanted it this way.'

A step back in time, he'd said, a chance to do things right.

She'd been hesitant at first, with so many spectacular venues in Melbourne for a wedding, but the moment they'd stepped into this place, hand in hand, she'd known.

It was meant to be.

The old nightclub on the shores of Albert Park Lake might have undergone renovations and a name change but, as they'd stepped out onto the balcony, memories had bombarded her, and when her fiancé had led her to the rail, enveloped her in his arms and kissed her the way she'd craved all those years ago, she couldn't think of any other place she'd rather get married.

'You're a pair of sentimental fuddy-duddies.' Mattie rolled her eyes, her smile soft. 'Can't wait to see what you do for your tenth anniversary.'

Slipping an arm around her friend's waist, Eve squeezed. 'Whatever it is, you and the other babes will be around to see it.'

Mattie's faux huff lasted all of two seconds. 'If you had to give us a nickname, I suppose we should be thankful we're babes.'

Eve laughed. 'Bryce never should've told you.'

Mattie held up her pinkie, wiggled it. 'You're

not the only one who has him wrapped around this. He's no match for all of us.'

'Poor guy.'

'You lovely ladies talking about me?'

Eve sighed and melted against her husband's solid chest as he slid his arms around her from behind.

'All good things.' Mattie winked. 'Now, some bossy events coordinator has given me a job to do, so I better go do it.'

'Thanks.'

As Mattie sashayed away, resplendent in her floor-length amethyst raw silk bridesmaid sheath, Eve turned in the circle of Bryce's arms.

'You've done an amazing job today.'

She tilted her head up, her eyes fluttering closed as Bryce brushed a tender kiss across her lips, an all-too-brief kiss if the tightening of his arms around her waist and the sudden flare of heat between them was any indication.

'It wasn't a job. It was a labour of love.'

'Our love.'

He trailed a fingertip down her cheek, across

her jaw, tracing her bottom lip. 'I love you, Mrs Gibson.'

He ducked his head, kissed her again, murmuring against the corner of her mouth, 'And, at the risk of repeating myself for the hundredth time, you look utterly ravishing.'

'What, this old thing?'

She glanced down at her tailor-made empire line gown in rich alabaster satin, her eyes widening even now, after a day of wearing the exquisite wedding gown. For, no matter how many times she saw herself in this stunning dress, she'd never get used to it.

Today, the bridesmaid had become the bride. And she couldn't be happier.

Resting his hand on her hip, Bryce's intense stare travelled down her body and back up, a slow, sensual perusal that left her in little doubt what would happen later when the gown slipped off.

'You know, as gorgeous as you look in this, it wouldn't have mattered what you wore today; you're always beautiful to me.'

Tears stung the back of her eyes, the power of

his simple declaration cradling her heart, rein-forcing how lucky she'd been to take a chance on this incredible man all these years later.

'So you wouldn't have cared if I'd shown up in a grungy T-shirt, daggy denim shorts and glasses?'

'Not a bit.'

'Bird's nest hair? No make-up? Jewellery-free?'

'Wouldn't matter.'

Laying a hand on his shoulder, she leaned forward, stood on tiptoe to whisper in his ear. 'In nothing at all?'

'Now you're talking.'

His arms tightened around her waist, his fierce hug saying more than words ever could.

Bryce Gibson loved her, whatever she wore, however she looked, the ultimate reassurance for the shy geek girl she'd once been, who'd taken full advantage of her Cinderella moment and morphed into a fully fledged bride.

'Follow me.'

He released her, slipped her hand in his and Eve knew she would follow this man wherever he led for the rest of her life.

They stepped out onto the balcony overhanging the lake, the Melbourne cityscape casting a mauve tinge against the night sky, moved to the furthest corner away from their guests.

She remembered this spot, remembered everything about that fateful night—the night that had ultimately led her here, to this moment, with this man.

Sliding his hands around her waist, Bryce tugged her close. 'We once talked about dreams in this very spot.'

'How could I forget?'

'I just wanted you to know that having you in my life, being married to you, has made mine come true.'

As he lowered his head, his lips warm and firm in a lingering kiss, she melded against him, secure in the knowledge she was finally living her dream too.

MILLS & BOON PUBLISH EIGHT LARGE PRINT TITLES A MONTH. THESE ARE THE EIGHT TITLES FOR SEPTEMBER 2010.

VIRGIN ON HER WEDDING NIGHT
Lynne Graham

BLACKWOLF'S REDEMPTION
Sandra Marton

THE SHY BRIDE
Lucy Monroe

PENNILESS AND PURCHASED
Julia James

BEAUTY AND THE RECLUSIVE PRINCE
Raye Morgan

EXECUTIVE: EXPECTING TINY TWINS
Barbara Hannay

A WEDDING AT LEOPARD TREE LODGE
Liz Fielding

THREE TIMES A BRIDESMAID…
Nicola Marsh

MILLS & BOON PUBLISH EIGHT LARGE PRINT TITLES A MONTH. THESE ARE THE EIGHT TITLES FOR OCTOBER 2010.

MILLS & BOON